THE BLACK PASSAGEWAY OF DEATH

With drumming pulses, my breath coming in quick short gasps, I stood silent as a thing of carven stone, searching the darkness with every sense for the slightest sign of my opponent's position.

I could not see or hear him, but I sensed his presence. My flesh prickled and my nape hairs stirred, as if with some sixth sense I registered the pressure of invisible eyes.

Then a beam of blinding light struck me full in the eyes—a naked steel blade flashed for my heart—and in the next instant I found myself fighting for my life. . . .

BLACK LEGION OF CALLISTO

LIN CARTER

A DELL BOOK

Published by
Dell Publishing Co., Inc.
1 Dag Hammarskjold Plaza
New York, New York 10017
Printed in the United States of America
First printing—December 1972
Second printing—February 1973
Third printing—January 1974

**Black Legion of
Callisto**
is dedicated to
CAMILLE CAZEDESSUS, JR.
and
the readers of "ERB-dom."

CONTENTS

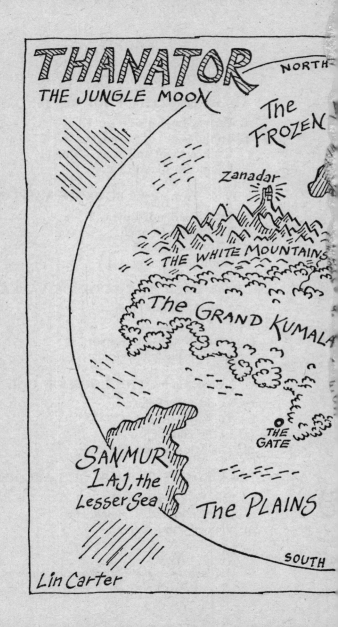

DIAMETER — 2770 m.
CIRCUMFERENCE — 8702 m.
4351 miles from pole to pole.

POLE

AND

Farz

ORUND IAJ

the Greater Sea

Narouk

Perushtar

anatol

Soraba

THE AJAND

Tharkol

Shondakor

THE SECRET VALLEY

of HARATHA

THE BLACK MOUNTAINS

POLE

KORADS

0   25 50 75 100 125 150

1 KORAD = 7 MILES

A FEW WORDS OF INTRODUCTION

The morning of January 5, 1970—a Monday—I went into the city to discuss a new contract with Henry Morrison, my agent, and to visit one of my publishers. Since I had gotten an early start, I concluded my business shortly after lunch and returned to my home on Long Island a little before three o'clock in the afternoon. My wife Noël met me at the door.

"Guess who called while you were out," she said, with an air of suppressed excitement in her voice.

"Sprague?"

"No—Gary Hoyt."

"Gary Hoyt!" I exclaimed in amazement. "Where did he call from? I didn't even know he was in the country!"

Noël grinned. "As a matter of fact, he hasn't been in the country for more than an hour or so," she explained. "He phoned about two, saying he had just arrived at Kennedy. I knew you'd be anxious to talk to him, so I invited him to dinner."

Frankly, there were very few human beings alive on the face of the globe that Monday afternoon with whom I was more interested in conversing. Gary Hoyt! He was my only link with a gallant young soldier of fortune named Jonathan Andrew Dark who had vanished in the jungles of Cambodia early in March of 1969. Hoyt, a major in the Air Force stationed in Saigon, had been Jon Dark's closest friend, and from his hands the previous November I had received a thick bundle of manuscript which purported

to be the first-person narrative of Jon Dark's amazing
adventures following his disappearance in the Cambodian jungles.

"Swell. But what'll he be doing between now and
dinner? Why couldn't we put him up in the Chinese
room? How long is he going to be in town?"

"Just a day or two," my wife said. "He had already
made a reservation at the Chelsea in Manhattan. I
took down the number. . . ."

Writers usually have a lot of friends they have never met—people who like their books so much that they
write a letter to the author, care of his publisher.
Sometimes a correspondence springs up, and author
and reader become friends without ever actually
meeting in person. This was how I knew Major Hoyt.
His friend, Jon Dark, was serving as commander of a
helicopter squadron flying mercy missions for the International Red Cross in South Vietnam. Billeted
together, the two had become close friends. Dark disappeared from human knowledge almost a year before
when his copter was forced down across the Cambodian border while his squadron was flying food, med-
ics, and supplies from a temporary field near Hon
Quan, which is about sixty-five miles north of Saigon
and only about ten miles from the border, to a small
village in the north which had been hard hit by Viet
Cong terrorists. The jungle area in which he disappeared is one of the densest and least explored jungles
on Earth, and routine search flights had discovered
neither the gallant young pilot nor the wreckage of
his helicopter.

But early in August of last year, Cambodian natives
had discovered a bundle of dilapidated manuscript
somewhere in the interior; a covering note had re-
quested the finder to deliver the manuscript to Hoyt
and assured that a reward would be paid. This manuscript, which was handwritten in some sort of homemade ink and inscribed with a quill pen on a crude

brownish paper resembling ancient papyrus, told an incredible story . . . and it was, if the word of its author can be accepted, a *true* story.

Captain Dark told of being forced down by engine troubles on a jungle river, of finding a ruined city and therein stumbling upon a mysterious well lined with strange milky translucent stone like Soochow jade. From the mouth of this well a beam of sparkling force thrust up against the star-jeweled jungle night. Accidentally coming into contact with this weird beam of radiance, Dark found himself miraculously transported to the surface of another world which the natives called "Thanator" but which he believed to be Callisto, the fifth moon of the planet Jupiter. The manuscript consisted of a narrative of his adventures and travels on the moon Callisto, and if we can accept the veracity of that account, it is the most fantastic true adventure in the annals of human experience.

Hoyt had forwarded the narrative to me on sheer whim. Dark, it seemed, had no family and no heirs to dispute this literary property, which the Major cautiously assumed to be a venture into fantastic fiction. Since both Jon Dark and Gary Hoyt had a mutual interest in sword and sorcery, and had enjoyed several of my own novels in the genre, Hoyt reasonably assumed I might be willing to pass judgment on the worthiness of this "novel," if that was all it was. In a covering letter, Gary Hoyt remarked that Dark, then missing in action a good five months and presumed dead, left no heirs and that I might do what I wished with the novel—keep it as a rather unique souvenir or even have it published. I found the novel splendidly exciting and well worthy of print, edited it into a typescript, and delivered it to Gail Morrison, my editress at Dell Books, who waxed enthusiastic over the story, purchased it, but insisted on using my name as author. I suspect that Gail did not and does not believe my account of receiving the manuscript anything more than an elaborate hoax. However, if the story be a hoax, it is not of my doing, and if Captain Jon Dark ever returns to this world he will find that I have banked the royalties in an escrow account under his name.

To the edited version of Captain Dark's manuscript I have given the title *Jandar of Callisto*—"Jandar" being the way the Callistan natives pronounced his name, Jon Dark.

The annoying and baffling thing about *Jandar of Callisto* is that Captain Dark left his story unfinished, its plot unresolved. Dell made no comment on this, assuming, I suppose, that I intended to follow it up with a sequel. The story breaks off at a suspenseful point. Jandar, who had rescued the Princess Darloona of Shondakor from a thousand perils, was struggling through a dense tract of Callistan jungle known as the Grand Kumala, attempting to make contact with Darloona's people, the Ku Thad, driven from their city by a bandit army known as the Black Legion. During the excitement of attack by a ferocious yathrib, a gigantic predator of the Callistan jungles, Jandar and Darloona were separated, and he later watched in helpless anxiety as she was taken, a bound prisoner, into the very stronghold of her foes, the Black Legion. At that point his narrative concluded, despairing of ever seeing again the woman he now realized he loved.

Frankly, that's a hell of a way to end a novel! It leaves the reader hanging in suspense. I briefly considered writing my own ending to the tale, but eventually decided this would not be proper: it was not so much a matter of believing the narrative to be a true record, for on this point I determined to keep an open mind. It was a question of my right to tamper with another man's work—that was the deciding factor.

Captain Dark explained that amidst the jungles he had encountered Darloona's warrior people and they had led him to the disk of milky jade, encircled by a ring of standing stones, which was the Callistan end

of the mysterious "transporter beam" which linked two
worlds. After completing the narrative of his adventures, he planned to place the manuscript in the path
of that beam of sparkling force, hoping that some account of his remarkable adventures and discoveries
on the jungle moon of Thanator would thus be returned to Earth. This would seem to be what had
happened, for according to later letters from Major
Hoyt, Cambodian hunters found the bundle of papyrus in a ruined city closely resembling the one which
Captain Dark had entered, and to which he had given
a name, calling it the Lost City of Arangkôr.

I had by this time exchanged several letters with
Gary Hoyt, and among other things I had informed
him of my intentions of publishing *Jandar of Callisto*.
Now, it seemed, we were at last to meet. I was curious
to discover just what sort of a man he was.

It was beyond the realm of possibility to prove
Dark's narrative either a work of fiction or a truthful
account of the most amazing adventure any man ever
lived. I had devoted a not inconsiderable amount of
effort and research to the solution of this problem,
and had, most infuriatingly, found evidence to support *both* answers.

An afternoon's conversation with astronomers at the
Hayden Planetarium disclosed that Callisto could not
possibly support the variety of life forms claimed by
the manuscript. While it is true that Callisto is one of
the larger satellites in our solar system, it could not
possibly have the earth-normal gravity and atmosphere Captain Dark describes because it is only a
fraction of the size of our planet. The authorities at
Hayden Planetarium were most definite on this point,
calling my attention to the very slight gravity experienced by the Apollo astronauts on our own Moon
whose diameter is only six hundred and seven miles
less than that of Callisto. The heroes of Apollo 11
found an arid desert world, virtually devoid of atmo-

sphere save for minute traces of such unbreathable gases as xenon and krypton, baked by the unshielded fury of the sun, frozen in the lunar night, with a gravity only a fraction of earth norm.

Conditions on the moon Callisto should be virtually identical, but much colder, since the fifth satellite of Jupiter is some three hundred and ninety million miles farther distant from the Sun. Frozen in perpetual night, surrounded by a hard vacuum, scoured eternally by life killing space radiation, Callisto could not possibly be the lush, fertile world Captain Dark describes.

It had, of course, occurred to me that the manuscript might actually be the work of Gary Hoyt. This I could neither prove nor disprove, but I could at least ascertain whether "Jon Dark" was an actual person or not. I found conclusive evidence, both from the United States government and the headquarters of the International Red Cross, that a Jonathan Andrew Dark had in fact disappeared on a mercy mission in Vietnam at the time and under the same conditions as the manuscript relates. This still proved little: the Major might well have used a friend as model for his character; hence, as you can imagine, I was very interested to meet him and to form my own opinion of his personality and truthfulness.

For, while there was much in *Jandar of Callisto* that was, if not intrinsically impossible, at least fantastic and unlikely, there was also an intriguing amount of corroborative detail in the manuscript that was, or could be, true. The approximate area of the Cambodian jungle into which he vanished *was* largely unexplored; lost and ruined cities, such as the one Captain Dark claimed to have discovered, *do* in fact exist— such as the colossal edifices of Angkor Vat farther to the north—and in a book called *Unsolved Mysteries of Asia,* written by a British archaeologist and explorer, Sir Malcolm Jerrolds, published in 1964 by Macmillan, I learned that native legends tell of a city in that same area, and that a Southeast Asian saga mentions it by the name of Arangkôr—the identical name which Dark used! With these facts in mind, I looked forward with eager anticipation to that evening and my first meeting with Gary Hoyt.

He was a tall, lean man in his early forties, tanned and fit and most distinguished in his Air Force blues, with steady gray eyes, a firm handshake, and a quiet, precise way of speaking. He apologized to my wife for any inconvenience his visit might have caused us, acknowledged the excited, yelping welcome of our five dogs—gravely shaking the huge paw our St. Bernard, Sir Dennis, extended—and dealt manfully with the superb roast beef dinner Noël had prepared, apologizing for the relish with which he tackled a second helping, saying this was the first home-cooked meal he had enjoyed in a long time.

Over coffee and liqueurs, the Major and I talked. His tour of duty in Vietnam was now over and he was en route to his family home in St. Paul, Minnesota. My wife had gone to college at the U of M, so they had common landmarks to discuss. While my wife and the Major talked, I looked him over thoughtfully. Like just about everyone else in the world, I pride myself on my ability to size up a man on first meeting, and everything about Major Hoyt—his quiet deep voice, his clear steady gaze, his gentlemanly manner —told me this was a man I could trust and believe in.

Moreover, he liked my dogs, and they liked him. That was enough for me!

Eventually, of course, we got around to Jon Dark. And here Gary Hoyt had some exciting news to surprise me with.

"Mr. Carter, I don't suppose you've ever heard of a fellow named Jerrolds—an Englishman, traveler and archaeologist, wrote a couple books on Southeast Asia?" he began. I repressed a start, for Jerrolds was the man in whose book I had found corroborative

evidence to support Jon Dark's discovery of the Lost
City of Arangkôr! I said as much and Gary Hoyt
nodded soberly.

"That's good," he said. "He was one of my profes-
sors at college, which is how I know of him. Ran into
him in Saigon just before Christmas. Well, I told him
about Jon's book, although I was careful to point out
that it was just a story and nothing more. He got
pretty excited when I told him how Jon said it was so
close to that jungle river where he crash-landed his
chopper—dug out some maps and showed me how the
Mekong makes a curve through that neck of the
woods. He said nobody ever hunted for the Lost City
down in that part of the country, because all of the
other ruined cities of the Khmer race were quite a bit
to the north, beyond the Tonle-Sap. That's a big lake
in central Cambodia, you know."

I nodded. "I've read about it, Major. Supposed to
be the last shrinking remnant of a mighty prehistoric
sea. Please go on—you've got my imagination working!"

He laughed. "I guess I got the Professor's imagination going, too! Because he said all of this confirmed
a theory he had been working up for years. Let me see
if I can get this straight, now. . . . Seems the natives
have queer old legends about a ruined city down in
the south, around where Jon said he found Arangkôr,
and they have some odd stories about it, too, in their
sagas. Story goes something like this: way back at the
beginning of time there was a great sorcerer-king of
the Khmer race, a fellow named Pra-Eun. Well, the
'gods' spoke to him and told him to gather all of his
people together and build a mighty city in the jungles,
and to set a big square plaza in the middle of it, with
a well in the exact center, and a ring of big statues,
and all—"

"—just like the scene in Captain Dark's book!" I
exclaimed.

He nodded. "They told him how to build this well

to certain specifications, and to line it with a certain rare stone. And when everything was finished, just like the gods had said, this Pra-Eun called all of his people together and they prayed, and a ray of light came down from heaven like a golden ladder and all the people marched up that ladder into the country of heaven—and that's what happened to the mysterious lost race we call the Khmer!"

He paused to take another sip of brandy and to ruffle the ears of my little brown dog, Molly, who was pawing his knee for attention.

"Well, to make a long story short, the Professor thought he had a good idea of the exact part of the country Jon was talking about, and he set out for it just a couple days after that. He was in Saigon on his way to Cambodia to join an expedition that was being recruited by some of his people—I guess I should have mentioned earlier on that he had left the U of M years ago, and was now on the staff of the Oriental Institute of Chicago, the people that organized all those expeditions to Egypt and dug up all those tombs. Well, I didn't expect to hear anything from him, and I was just about to get out of the service anyway, and thinking about getting back home, but just before I left, he sent me—"

Here he paused again, to open up the small leather attaché case that had never left his side since he first entered my house. He drew something out and handed it to me.

"—this!"

I stared down, with a mixture of delight and astonishment, at a thick sheaf of crude brown papyrus covered with small neat handwriting inscribed with a quill pen in homemade ink. *A manuscript identical in every respect with the first book of Jandar's narrative!*

"He found Arangkôr, then," I breathed.

"He found it. And the plaza, and the ring of statues, and the jade well that Jon calls 'the Gate Between The

Worlds.' And in the bottom of the well—this manuscript, just like the other one."

Major Hoyt left the city a day or two later, promis-
ing to keep in touch, and I settled down to the exciting task of reading the second installment of
Jandar's adventures on the moon Callisto—the same
story I have published here.

As before, I have not tampered with the narrative,
save to do a little editorial tinkering with the grammar and punctuation, to give titles to the chapters,
and to provide a few explanatory footnotes which I
have signed with my initials. We have reproduced my
redrawn version of the Callisto map which adorned
the first Jandar book, since the scenery is the same in
this volume of his history.

Also as before, the story breaks off without the full
story having resolved itself. Whether or not any further word will arrive from the unknown depths of
space is a matter I cannot answer. But I have written
to Sir Malcolm Jerrolds, who is still engaged in the
work of excavation, cataloging and exploring the ruins
of the Lost City of Arangkôr, and he confirms the account of the discovery of the manuscript in every
particular.

In a few months, my wife and I had planned to
take a short vacation. We had been thinking of En-
gland, but right now Noël is looking at some literature
from Trans-World Airlines to see what flights they
provide to Cambodia. Sir Malcolm has invited us to
visit the dig, if we are in that part of the world. And,
in all truthfulness, I dream of seeing the aeon-old towers of lost and legended Arangkôr loom up against
the mystery of the jungle night, and of seeing with my
own eyes that flickering beam of uncanny radiance
from within the jade mouth of the well that is the
Gate Between The Worlds . . . wherethrough passed
many months ago a daring young adventurer, bound
on the most fantastic journey known to the annals of

exploration, to face ten thousand perils on an unknown world of magic and beauty and terror.

Shall I ever know the truth of the tale? Or will it
exploration, to face ten thousand perils on an unsolved mysteries of the Earth?

Time will tell. . . .

—LIN CARTER

Hollis, Long Island, New York
January 20, 1970

BOOK ONE

THE BOOK OF JANDAR

CHAPTER ONE

YARRAK, LORD OF THE KU THAD

It is one of the more remarkable of the verities of life that in many circumstances one man can accomplish that which thousands would find impossible.

I refer to the means by which I achieved the solution of my dilemma.

Through the action of a mysterious force, whose nature was still an inexplicable enigma, I had been transported across the tremendous gulf of space which yawns between the planet of my birth and Callisto, moon of Jupiter.

No sooner had I materialized on the surface of that strange and beautiful world of black and crimson jungles, whose queer skies of golden vapor are lit by enormous moons, than I found myself thrust into the midst of adventures beyond parallel in human history.

Alone and friendless in an alien world of curious peoples and ferocious monsters, that I managed to survive unscathed I owe to a mixture of audacity, chance, and accident, rather than courage or wisdom.

I found a primitive world torn by savage antagonisms, where the hand of every man was lifted in eternal enmity against every other. Three races of sentient beings, each distinctly differing from the other, had I thus far encountered during my wandering adventures across the face of the jungle moon.

Lowest in the scale of civilization was the Yathoon Horde, a primitive nation of warrior clans. The Yathoon are not human beings, are not, in fact, even remotely hominid, but a peculiar species of arthropod.

Like tall, jointed insect-men they seem, their gaunt
yet not ungraceful limbs clad in sheaths of gray chitin,
their faces mere featureless masks of glistening horny
substance adorned with quivering antennae, their eyes
somber and expressionless orbs of jeweled blackness,
their clacking and metallic voices devoid of inflection.
Naked, seemingly sexless, the stalking monstrosities
live lives of endless warfare and know nothing of the
finer sensibilities: love, paternity, friendship, mercy—
all the emotions which adorn the human soul are unknown to them.

At first I feared the uncanny arthropods and found
them loathsome. But eventually, during the months of
my captivity in which I was not mistreated, I came to
understand the poor creatures and to sympathize with
their cold, lonely lives. I found them no longer ugly or
repellent; their stalking, multijointed limbs assumed
the functional perfection of a beautifully designed machine, their gaunt skeletal figures the elongated beauty
of an attenuated sculpture by Giacometti.

At length I succeeded in making my first friend
upon Thanator, which is the name by which the natives of Callisto call their mysterious world. This
individual, a chieftain named Koja, to whom I be-
longed, proved susceptible to the finer emotions once
their practical utility was demonstrated to him. I
saved his life when the indifference of his fellow warriors would have left him to die, and in so doing I
placed him under a certain obligation, for the Yathoon
are not without a primitive code of honor and are
cognizant of indebtedness (which they call *uhorz*).
Ere long he reciprocated my kindness by releasing
me from my involuntary servitude.

And thus, in my new freedom, I encountered the
second of the higher races of Thanator, for I chanced
to rescue from the attack of a savage dragon-cat, or
yathrib, a beautiful girl named Darloona. She was the
reigning princess of a walled stone city, Shondakor,
whose people, the Ku Thad, had but recently been

driven into exile by a bandit army. The Ku Thad
are fully human and represent a higher level of civilization than that yet achieved by the poor arthropods.
In appearance they resemble an unlikely combination
of Southeast Asian and Nordic racial features, with
their honey-amber skin, slanted emerald eyes, and
curly red-gold manes. Seized by a rival Yathoon chieftain, one Gamchan, and condemned to torment, we
were freed by my friend Koja, only to fall into the
clutches of yet another race.

This race, the Sky Pirates, as they are called, represent the most advanced civilization on all of Thanator. They dwell in a mountaintop city called Zanadar,
whose lofty elevation would render it inaccessible
save for their remarkable and ingenious flying ships,
which are unlike any form of aerial vehicle ever perfected upon Earth and demonstrate an astonishing
level of technological ingenuity. The Sky Pirates differ
from the Ku Thad in their papery-white flesh, lank
black hair, and Caucasoid features.

The cunning and unscrupulous monarch of the Sky
Pirates, Prince Thuton, condemned me to slavery while
pretending to befriend Darloona. I won freedom,
and found a friend among the Zanadarians in the person of Master Lukor, a gallant and gentlemanly master swordsman who taught me the skills and secrets of
his craft. Learning that Thuton was secretly negotiating with Darloona's deadliest foe, the bandit chief
who had overwhelmed her city, Lukor, Koja, and I
effected our escape from the City in the Clouds by
means of one of the ingenious flying contraptions.

Injured in a gale, the flying machine crashed in
a mighty zone of dense jungles called the Grand
Kumala. Although we had escaped the wreck without
harm, our party was attacked by one of the savage
predators of the jungle and the Princess Darloona became separated from us and was taken prisoner by a
bandit patrol. Helpless to render aid, we watched
from the margin of the jungle as she was borne a

prisoner into her own city of Shondakor.

Wandering in the jungles, we eventually encountered her people, the Ku Thad, and joined forces with them.

Although the Ku Thad were able to direct me to the mysterious Gate Between The Worlds, whereby I had first come to this barbaric world, I elected to remain behind, for I realized at last that I was hopelessly in love with the flame-haired beauty of Darloona. I employ the word "hopeless" to describe my suit, and for excellent reason. Not only did it seem impossible that I should ever see her again, but even were such to occur, she would coldly spurn my affections, for the proud, fiery Princess had conceived a misapprehension concerning me, and deemed me a coward, a weakling, and virtually an enemy.

At an impasse, helpless to rescue the woman I loved from her captivity, I set down an account of my adventures on Thanator, feeling that some narrative of my remarkable discoveries, however crudely composed, should be preserved. This manuscript I placed within the Gate, hoping that it should thus be transported to the far-distant planet of my birth. It was with mixed emotions that I observed it as it disappeared in the weird beam of sparkling force. Whether or not it safely traversed the colossal distances between the worlds, to reach the surface of Earth at last, I shall probably never know.

Shondakor was in the grip of a wandering bandit host known as the Chac Yuul—the Black Legion— who had taken the city by surprise or treachery some months before.

I am at a loss to find any parallel in terrene history for this bandit legion. A large and disciplined force of fighting men, homeless nomads, willing on the one hand to sell their swords as mercenaries in any conflict between opposed cities, and on the other, to seize by force lands or loot, they are uniquely Thanatorian. I suppose the closest parallels could be found in the nomadic warrior clans of seventeenth-century Russia, such as the Don Cossacks. Then again, in certain characteristics the Black Legion resembles the wandering bands of *condottieri* found in fifteenth-century Italy.

Professional warriors, forswearing homeland and family, banded together under a military commander selected by popular acclaim, they go where they will, living off the land, here attacking a merchant caravan, there seizing a fishing village or a farming hamlet, sometimes laying siege to the castle of some wealthy aristocrat, at other times selling their swords as a mercenary unit in some internecine conflict. What had led them to assault one of the most splendid and brilliant of all the great cities of this world was still an unsolved mystery, but they had seized control of the metropolis in a blitzkrieg attack. Perhaps their warlord, Arkola, wearied of the rude nomadic life of camp and march and yearned to wield power over a kingdom of his own.

The enemy already within the gates, the Princess of Shondakor chose a reckless expedient and led many of her people forth to the freedom of the open plains, rather than attempt the defense of the city, which would have resulted in a massacre. The class of warrior nobility which followed her into self-imposed exile did not unanimously favor her decision, but they venerated their gorgeous and high-spirited princess, the descendant of a thousand kings, and at length were persuaded as to the truth of the old adage, "he who fights and runs away, lives to fight another day."

Now bereft of their princess, the leadership of the Ku Thad had devolved upon the stout shoulders of Lord Yarrak, Darloona's uncle. He was a tall, stately, martial leader with a natural ability for command. When Lukor, Koja, and I were first brought before him and he learned of the various assistances we had rendered to his niece and queen, he welcomed us with

great honor and hospitality. And thus for weeks we
had lived with the Ku Thad warriors amid the trackless jungles of the Grand Kumala.

These jungles covered literally thousands of square
miles and in their density and tracklessness afforded
the Shondakorians the most perfect hiding place imaginable. The Black Legion warriors had never pursued
the exiled nobles, not caring what became of them so
long as they presented no menace.

And indeed they did not. Although the Ku Thad
were stalwart and courageous fighting men, and although they hungered to free their captive nation
from their bandit overlords, they were too few in
number to offer the Chac Yuul a challenge. The Shondakorians totaled no more than two or three thousand,
and the Black Legion could summon to arms three
times their number. Also, the walls of the city were
monumental, and their girth immense. So huge a metropolis was Shondakor that it would take an army of
no less than ten thousand warriors to effectively lay
siege and block all gates and exits. The irony of our
situation lay in this trick of fate, that it had been the
ancestors of the Ku Thad who had, with infinite labor
and over scores of years, raised those strong walls
which now formed an impassable barrier to their own
descendants.

Night after night around the council fires we discussed the ways and means whereby we might suc-
cessfully wrest Shondakor from her conquerors. The
great many-colored moons of Thanator gazed down
on our fruitless arguments and vain discussions, and
the problem remained unsolved when the vaporous
golden skies paled with the sudden flare of the Thanatorian dawn.

Overwhelming force of arms might have breached
the walls, but our numbers were insufficient.

A surprise attack might well gain us entry through
one of the less well-guarded gates, but our very small-
ness of number made it hard to see how we could

manage to overcome so great a force as would then oppose us.

Eventually, I conceived of a desperate plan.

It had one chance in a thousand of success.

I would attempt to enter the gates of Shondakor alone!

Yarrak regarded me with an expression generally reserved for the ravings of a madman.

"Jandar, no one doubts your courage or cunning, but what can one man possibly do against so many?"

"He can do one thing alone, which would be impossible to a number," I replied. "He can get in."

"I do not follow your reasoning," he admitted.

"Simply this. The Black Legion guards would hardly permit two thousand armed warriors to enter the gates without a pitched battle. But one man will enter easily and without opposition. Because they will feel the same as you—what can one man do against them?"

My old friend, Lukor the Swordmaster, instantly realized the truth of my observation.

"And, once within, you will have considerable freedom and an opportunity, at least, to see what can be done towards freeing the Princess!" he suggested.

"Even so," I nodded.

Lord Yarrak considered the matter in silence. "But why should they admit you at all?" he asked at length.

I shrugged. "Why not? I am not of the Ku Thad race, as my tan skin, yellow hair, and blue eyes freely attest. A Ku Thad seeking entry would arouse suspicions, but I will not. I will present myself in disguise as a wandering mercenary seeking entry into their ranks. The Chac Yuul are not a race, a nation, or a clan, but a free association of fighting men from every corner of Thanator, brought together through a common desire for loot. A solitary warrior should have no great difficulty in gaining access to their host."

Yarrak smiled, his troubled face clearing.

"I must confess myself reluctantly persuaded to the strength of your plan," he said, "although I still question whether one man behind the city walls can aid our plans in any way."

"One agent within the walls can do more than *no* agent within the walls, my lord," Lukor pointedly observed.

Yarrak laughed and admitted the truth of that statement.

"I shall wear the simple leather tunic of a common warrior," I said, "and bear unmarked steel. The most they can do is turn me away. But if they do not, then I have a fighting chance of winning a place in their army, and, in time, perhaps of affording the Princess some opportunity of escape."

"You will need a covering story, to account for yourself," mused Lord Yarrak, falling in with my plan. "You could say you had been a mercenary swordsman in the service of Soraba, which is a city of the north. The Chac Yuul have not been in the north for ten years, so you will run no danger of having the details of your account brought into question."

"My lord, Jandar may find some difficulty because of his unusual coloring," spoke up wise old Zastro, a sage elder of the Ku Thad who had been listening to our discussion.

"I shall tell them simply that I am a traveler from a far distant land," I said, "which is nothing more than the truth."

They smiled at this, for of course they knew my story, and my remark, although true, was something of an understatement. For my homeland was three hundred and eighty-seven million, nine hundred and thirty thousand miles away—"far distant" indeed!

"I do not think you should go into this danger alone, Jandar," said Koja in his solemn way. The gallant old Swordmaster nodded in vigorous assent.

"I could not agree with friend Koja more," he said. "Together, the two of us—"

"The *three* of us—" added Koja.

"Thanks, but I think one man has a better chance of getting in, than three," I said firmly.

"But—"

"I am young enough, and a fair-enough swordsman, to pass myself off as a landless, penniless mercenary," I pointed out. "But you, Lukor, are a master in the art of fence, and a most distinguished gentleman in your appearance, taste, and manner. It would be hard going to convince the suspicious Chac Yuul that any gentleman of your evident sophistication and sense of honor is a wandering sell-sword rogue. And, Koja, when have the noble chieftains of the Yathoon clans enlisted with the Black Legion bandits? No, friends, I thank you. But this adventure is mine alone."

There were several further arguments to be thrashed out, but in the end it was decided to my satisfaction. I would leave at dawn.

CHAPTER TWO

TO THE GATES OF SHONDAKOR

The dawns of Callisto—or Thanator, as I should accustom myself to thinking of this jungle world—are a unique experience. They have to be seen to be believed.

Thanator, the fifth moon of Jupiter, literally has no sun. In common with the rest of the twelve moons of the giant planet, it is so very distant from the central luminary of our solar system that the sun seems but the brightest of the stars visible in its skies.

By all rights, I suppose that the surface of Callisto should be a cold and airless waste of dead, frozen stone, drenched in perpetual gloom, illuminated only by the dim reflected glory of the Jove-light, for that mightiest of the planets bulks enormous in its skies. The above description doubtless tallies with the sober and considered pronouncements of terrene science.*

* Captain Dark is quite correct in making this assumption. I have consulted with astronomers at New York's Hayden Planetarium, and they have assured me that Callisto cannot possibly support any indigenous life forms above the level of certain hardy lichens. The satellite, which is more than five times farther away from the sun than is our own Earth, receives a correspondingly diminished fraction of the solar warmth and illumination which makes life on our planet a possibility. This would seem to definitely rule out the chances of Captain Dark's narrative being a factual rather than a fictional document. I inquired if it were not possible that Callisto had a molten core of temperature such as to render the surface tolerable to life, and learned that the authorities consider the moon far too small for this to be possible.—L.C.

But in fact, Callisto enjoys a gravity only fractionally less than that of my home world; and however impossible it may be, according to the currently accepted dogmas of science, Thanator is a warm and even tropic world, teeming with fecund life.

The skies of this jungle moon are composed of breathable vapors whose composition seems to me identical with that of Earth's own atmosphere (if this were not so, then how could I breathe it and continue to live?) with just one rather peculiar difference.

And that difference is the sky itself.

For high in the stratosphere of the Thanatorian atmosphere a layer of strange golden mist may be seen. Indeed, the skies of jungle-clad Thanator are not azure, but a glowing amber!

Dawn on Thanator is a sudden, sourceless brightening of this dome of golden vapor, which changes from complete darkness to a full and noonlike brilliance in just a matter of minutes.

This peculiar illuminative effect extends uniformly across the entire dome of the heavens, and it does not "rise" in the east and "set" in the west. I have never found a satisfactory answer to this phenomenon, but many are the mysteries of Thanator, and this is but one more.

All night we had traveled north through the Kumala, until shortly before dawn we were some distance north of Shondakor. Here I bade my comrades an affectionate farewell. From this point I must go forward alone in the face of whatever perils the unknown future held for me.

I traversed the plains to the shores of the river Ajand, forded the river, and came to a stone-paved highway which Lord Yarrak had called to my attention; from thence I turned south and rode for Shondakor. Since my story would have it that I came from Soraba, which is on the southern shore of the inland sea of Corund Laj, it would not do were I to approach the city from any direction but the north. I rode steadily, while the golden sky flushed suddenly with brilliance above me and bathed all of the level plains round about with noontime light.

My steed was a thaptor, a beast used by the natives of Callisto in place of the horse, which is unknown upon this world. In fact, mammals of any description are exceedingly rare upon Thanator, I have noticed.

Thaptors are wingless, four-legged avians. They resembled nothing so much as an unlikely hybrid of bird and horse, and whenever I see one I am irresistibly reminded of old Earth legends of the hippogriff,* for the thaptor might well have modeled for this fabulous creature. It is about the size of a large horse, but has clawed bird-feet, is clad in feathers, which rise in a manelike ruff just behind its head. Its beaked head and staring eyes bear a marked resemblance to the parrot.

The thaptors are unruly and restive and have never been completely domesticated, which makes riding one of them partake of the element of an adventure. Indeed, a mounted Thanatorian warrior habitually carries, strapped to his saddle, a small wooden club called an *olo* wherewith to crack his mount soundly atop the head should it seek to dislodge him from his place, or strive to crane its neck around and bite out a portion of his leg. This last habit of the thaptor makes me puzzle that the Thanatorians seem never to

---

* I fear Captain Dark has confused the gryphon with the hippogriff in this comparison. Thaptors are beaked, wingless but feathered, quadrupeds. The gryphon, described by classical authors such as Pliny, is a hybrid of eagle and lion, beaked and feathered. But the hippogriff is merely a winged horse, and beyond its feathered pinions bears no relation to the bird. At any rate, the hippogriff is not correctly termed a "legendary" beast, as it was an invention of the Italian poet, Ludovico Aristo, and first appears in world literature in his heroic romance, the *Orlando Furioso,* a production of the Renaissance. —L.C.

have invented the riding boot.

In their jungle home, the Ku Thad have little use for thaptors, but retain a few whereby their messengers can travel more rapidly than on foot. Thus it was that Yarrak was able to lend me a mount: it would have aroused needless suspicions in the breasts of the Black Legion had I arrived before their gates unmounted, claiming to have traversed the many miles of road from Soraba on foot.

After an hour of hard riding I came within sight of Shondakor.

The great city of the Ku Thad rose amidst the Plains of Haratha, on the eastern shore of the river. It was a splendid metropolis. The massive ramparts of its mighty wall encircled the city; tall spires rose in the brilliant morning light, and I could see the domes of palaces and mansions. All was built of stone, and the outer walls were faced with plaster that gleamed pale golden—hence its appellation, the "Golden City."

As I rode down to the gates of the walled stone city, I could not help feeling like some heroic warrior in a Sword and Sorcery novel. I'm sure I straightened my back, threw out my shoulders, and let my hand rest on the pommel of my sword in a swashbuckling manner.

Somewhat to my surprise, the gates were open and a number of farmers were passing through, leading carts and wagons filled with bags of grain, sides of meat, sacks of vegetables, and the like. This, I soon realized, was market day and the farmers from the surrounding countryside were bringing their goods to the bazaar. Ahead of me, as I joined the line filing through the gates, I saw warriors of the Chac Yuul negligently waving the peasants through the portals. Wheels creaked, dust swirled, and the heavy wagons clattered over the stone pavement. They were drawn by a species of draft animals unfamiliar to me—a heavy, lumbering beast with a thick short tail and a massive head, beaked, and horned, which looked like some ungainly cross between rhinoceros and triceratops.

I observed with a touch of wry humor that evidently life must go on, even in a conquered city which lay in the grip of its enemies. Farmers must sell their produce at market, housewives must purchase them, and men must eat, the rise and fall of dynasties notwithstanding.

I joined the end of the line and rode slowly towards the moment of decision. Would I be permitted to enter the city of the Chac Yuul, or would I be challenged?

As I approached the gates I felt the eyes of the guards upon me. One of them, a flat-faced, Mongollike little warrior with bandy legs and long, apelike arms, gestured me to a halt.

"You, there! Where do you think you are going?"

I looked down at him from the height of my saddle.

"Since this path leads only within the city, you should be able to figure out the answer to that question yourself," I replied calmly. Some urge of inner deviltry inspired the mocking insolence of my manner. I do not know whether or not it was wise, but it aroused a chorus of laughter from the bowlegged guard's comrades. His swarthy cheeks flushed and his eyes went cold.

"Get down off that thaptor," he snarled.

"Certainly. But I will still be taller than you, even when dismounted," I smiled. He flushed again, and again the hooting mockery of his comrades stung him. He turned on them.

"You—Calcan! Fetch the komad," he snarled. Then, displaying a vicious little hooked dagger, he said in a cold, level warning voice: "The next one of you *horeb* to laugh will kiss this."

They fell silent.

A horeb is a repulsive, wriggling rodent, a scaven-

ger of loathsome habits, not the least of which is that
it feeds off rotting garbage.

I waited, standing quietly, ready for anything. My
hands swung easily at my sides, only a fingerbreadth
from the pommel of sword and dagger. The bandy-
legged little guard eyed me with cold malevolence
and spat into the road dust eloquently.

"What's the trouble here?" a deep voice boomed.

A burly-shouldered, hulking Black Legion warrior
strode through the gates, to look over our little
tableau.

"It's this fellow here, Captain Bluto," the bandy-
legged little guard who had challenged me at the gate
whined, cocking a thumb in my general direction. "He
wants to get in the city, but he wears weapons, which
is against the rule."

Bluto looked me up and down with a squinting
eye. He was truly enormous, one of the tallest men I
have ever seen, and he literally towered over the other
Chac Yuul guardsmen, who tended to shortness on
the average. And he looked to be every bit as tough
and as strong as he was big. I felt an inward qualm.

Then I caught the look in the little bandy-legged
guard's eye. It was a smirk. I could read his thought
clearly: let's see you crack wise in front of Bluto, he
was thinking. I straightened my shoulders. In for a
penny, in for a pound.

"So you want to get in the city," Bluto grunted. He
rubbed a black-stubbled jaw with one hand the size
of a ham. Truly he was an enormous specimen of
manhood, although, I suspected, an abnormal specimen. I thought I detected in his underslung, progna-
thous jaw and the swollen muscles of his broad
shoulders, deep chest, and heavy legs the signs of a
glandular malfunction.

"That's right," I agreed. "Why all this? If a bunch
of mere peasants can troop in, who is to stop a trained
and experienced fighting man?"

Bluto grinned nastily, and a hot eager glint came into his eyes. Instantly I had him pegged for a bully. Most big men I have known were extraordinarily gentle; it was as if with their unusual size and strength went an obligation not to swagger it before less burly men than themselves. Not so with Bluto, I guessed. He delighted in crushing a man smaller than himself.

"So, he's a fighting man, is he?" he chuckled coarsely. And he began striding around me, looking me up and down with mock admiration. Then he looked a trifle disgruntled. His broad humor would have been more appropriate if I had been a lesser man myself, but I am considered rather tall and I believe I may truthfully state that the past months of action and adventure I had come through amidst the thousand perils of this jungle world had developed my musculature to a superb degree.

"In this city there are no fighting men but warriors of the Chac Yuul," he growled. I nodded amicably.

"So I have been given to understand. It is for that reason that I am here—to join forces with the Black Legion," I said.

He gave a belch of crude laughter. "The Black Legion! So, you think you are worthy to stand and fight by our side, eh? A little fellow like you?"

His men chuckled, but their humor was forced. For, in all truth, I must have looked rather prepossessing to men of their dwarfed stature, even when standing beside Bluto.

He slapped his arms and thumped his chest. "You think men like me need you to defend them?" he demanded, obviously working himself up into a fighting rage. Doubtless the poor lout's single pleasure lay in showing off his prowess before his warriors.

"I may not be as tall a man as yourself," I said with a cool, level glance, "but I have a long arm," and here I indicated the rapier that swung at my side.

"Give it to him, Komad," the bandy-legged little

guard leered. "Show him how a Chac Yuul swordsman deals with braggarts!"

Bluto was breathing heavily now, his dark face flushed, his brows congested. "You want to fight Bluto? You want to see what it takes to measure up to a Black Legion warrior?"

"I would prefer to save my fighting for the enemies of the Chac Yuul," I said. "To whom should I apply for enlistment?" And I made as if to step past him. He let loose with a bull-like roar and, reaching out, seized me by the upper arm and swung me about so that I faced him again.

"Stand still little man, when Bluto is talking to you —*uhh!*"

That gasp with which his bellow ended is easily explained. I dislike being handled, so I broke his hold with a karate chop that must have numbed him from elbow to wrist.

With an inarticulate roar, he struck me across the face!

I staggered—more shaken by surprise and astonishment than actually hurt by the clumsy blow.

My foot slipped and I went down on one knee.

A deathly silence had fallen over the thronged guards.

I felt my heart sink within me. Not that this noisy braggart worried me, for I was well aware that my skills with the sword were superior to anything this oafish bully could bring against me. But it had been my hope to enter the city of Shondakor without attracting any attention to myself. And nothing was more likely to bring me to the attention of the Lords of the Black Legion than a display of superb swordsmanship before their very gates, by one who pretended to be nothing more than just another ordinary mercenary!

Those hopes were dashed now, for it was unlikely

that I would be able to get past this Bluto without a fight.

Cursing the luck, I rose to my feet again and brushed the road dust from my garments while my mind raced furiously, striving to think of a way out of this dilemma.

CHAPTER THREE

I WIN A FIGHT
AND MAKE A FRIEND

There was no way to avoid the conflict, for a blow had been given and heated words had been exchanged.

Bluto stood there before me, legs spread, one hand hanging by the pommel of his sword. He was breathing heavily, his coarse features flushed, his little piglike eyes gleaming with fury.

"Draw your steel, man," he growled. "Let Bluto see what sort of a man you are and what your guts are made of."

I kept my hand well away from my blade, and with some difficulty I retained a calm smile.

A flash of excitement lit his little glinting eyes. I think he thought he faced a coward, and the bully within him heated to excitement at the thought. But this, also, was not the way out—for a coward would not be welcome in the ranks of the Black Legion.

Suddenly an inspiration occurred to me. I relaxed, breathing easily. For there was after all one mode of combat in which I could display superior prowess without arousing suspicion in those who were soon to be my superior officers.

"Well? What are you waiting for, you horeb?" he snarled.

I smiled and stood calmly, letting all see that I was at my ease.

"I presume even a band of ruffians such as yourselves has some conception of warriors' honor, and that a man struck in the face has the right to defend himself without charge of treason, riot, or insurrection," I remarked.

Bluto nodded, grunting. "Draw steel," he growled. "No man will speak against you. This is between the two of us."

"Very well," I said evenly. "If this is between we two alone, then it is a duel, and, being such, is under the code of honor. As the challenged, I have the right to choose weapons, and, as I prefer not to sully my steel with the vile gore of a bully and a coward, I choose—*fists!*"

Balling a fist, I swung a firm right and caught him in the pit of the stomach with every ounce of strength in arm, shoulder, and back. He was not anticipating such a blow, and the muscles of his abdomen were slack. Thus my balled fist struck his middle with an audible smack, like a butcher's mallet smacking a side of meat. My fist sank into his guts a good two inches.

His mouth drooped slackly; his face went sallow; he swayed, the heavy sword dropping from loose fingers to clang against the stony pave. He regarded me with a look of blank astonishment in his little piglike eyes.

Then I followed with a right to the jaw that must have broken a tooth or two. He bounced backwards, lifted a couple of inches off the ground by the impact of my blow, and fell with his back in the dust with a terrific thump and clatter of accouterments. And he did not get up again. He was out cold.

The fine art of fisticuffs, I should perhaps note here, is all but unknown on Thanator. It is not that pugilism is despised as an ungentlemanly mode of combat. It is, simply, that it has yet to be invented. And a man who knows how to use his fists is never without a weapon on this world.

Thus my conquest of their bully must have seemed almost magical in the eyes of the other guards. They gaped in amazement as I dusted my fingers together, and stepped across the prone Bluto, and led my steed through the gates of the city.

Not a man among them raised his voice in protest. And thus, at last, I entered the city of my princess.

The quiet voice of a tall, gentlemanly young man accosted me as I passed the gates.

"That was indeed well done, stranger," he smiled. "I believe I heard you express a desire to join the Chac Yuul. If that still holds true, permit me to guide you to the man to whom you should speak. For, in my estimate, the Black Legion has a place within its ranks for any warrior who can lay out the likes of Bluto with his bare hands!"

I laughed. "In my country, friend, we have a saying, which holds true, it seems, even in Shondakor. 'The bigger they are, the harder they fall.'"

He was amused by my quotation and offered me his hand. "I am Valkar of Ganatol, a *komor* of the third cohort," he said.

A *komor* is a chieftain, the leader of a cohort of warriors, which meant that my new-found friend was an officer of some importance in the Black Legion. I looked him over and liked what I saw. He was tall and trimly built, with dark skin, black hair, and green eyes—an odd combination I had not before come across during my adventures on Thanator; doubtless a half-breed, although he had the bearing of a noble or at least a gentleman of good family. His features were regular without being handsome to the point of prettiness, and he had a strong jaw, a good smile, and frank eyes. I liked him on sight.

I have discovered that I possess the unusual ability to measure a man's qualities almost on first meeting, and I can make up my mind on a man's honor and trustworthiness in moments after meeting him. This rare ability has saved my life ere now, and I have come to trust it. Hence I extended my hand to Valkar and we were friends from that moment to this, and will be friends, I trust, until Death, the great Dissolver of Companionships, comes between us at the end.

"I thank you for your friendly words," I said, clasping his hand in a firm grip. "My name is Jandar."

He eyed my blond hair, tan skin, and blue eyes with frank curiosity.

"Never have I seen a man with your coloring," he admitted. "May I ask of what nation you are a citizen?"

"The United States of America, a far-distant land," I said, and this was no more than the truth, as my country was at that moment distant by some nearly four hundred million miles, which I believe qualifies as "far."

Valkar repeated the name, stumbling a little over the unfamiliar sounds. Then he shook his head. "It must be on the other side of Thanator, for never have I heard of it before, nor met a man from there."

"That is quite understandable," I said. "For it is my belief that I am the first of my people to travel in these lands." This also, of course, was no more than the truth.

My new friend guided me through the streets of Shondakor to the citadel of the Black Legion. And as we conversed I took the opportunity to familiarize myself with the city. While Shondakor had been conquered by the Chac Yuul some months before, their new rulers seemed to reign with a light hand over the people of the city, for I saw citizens going about their business, opening their shops, conversing in the forum, purchasing goods in the bazaar, with a freedom of movement that denoted that the occupation of alien troops had imposed few limitations upon the natives.

The city was large and impressive, the buildings imposing and splendid edifices. Broad avenues lined with flowering trees were busy with traffic. Chariots clattered by, drawn by matched teams of finely bred thaptors. Wealthy merchants and their women went by in veiled palanquins supported on the shoulders of husky slaves. Urchins played and squabbled shrilly in the mouths of alleys, tattered and noisome beggars whined from doorways, Chac Yuul warriors spent their off-duty hours lounging in wineshops. The daily life of the city obviously went forward undisturbed, despite the change of dynasty.

The commandant of recruits—I shall not bore my readers, if any, with the title of this officer in the original Thanatorian—was a busy man, and since the *komor* Valkar vouched for me, I was signed up and sworn in without delay or undue questioning. I gave my most recent place of service as the city of Soraba on the shores of Corund Laj, and gave as the reason for my leaving the service of the Quraan of Soraba a quite natural disgruntlement at the preference given to nobles of family connection over common-born warriors of superior command and combat ability, such as myself. This may have seemed a trifle immodest of me, but I guessed that among a bandit horde such as the Chac Yuul the usual gentlemanly code of self-depreciation, common to the other fighting men of Thanator, would be absent and that a man would be taken more or less at his own estimate.

This seemed to have been an accurate guess on my part. At any rate, within the hour I was a full-fledged warrior of the Black Legion, assigned, at my own request, to the cohort that lay under the command of my new friend, Valkar of Ganatol.

And thus I had accomplished the first part of my plan, and had managed to enter the city and join the forces of my enemy.

As for the remainder of my plan, only time would tell if luck and accident would conspire to permit me the opportunity of rescuing the woman to whom I had given my heart.

I JOIN THE BLACK LEGION

And it was thus that I, Jandar of Callisto, entered upon my new career as a lowly warrior in the Black Legion, under the command of my newest friend, Valkar of Ganatol.

The third cohort, over which my friend was commander, was housed in a crude barracks along the southern side of a broad square or plaza which was called the Forum of Zeltadar. I later learned that the forum derived its name from the king of some remote era, an ancestor of Darloona's dynasty.

The common warriors, myself among them, slept in one enormous room upon flat, hard pallets which, during the hours of daylight, were rolled up and hung out of the way on hooks riveted to the wooden walls of the building.

We customarily arose at dawn, and upon those days when guard duty was not assigned to our cohort, we trained in the great Forum under the sharp eye of our commander, Valkar. And I soon came to understand that there is much, oh very much more to being a soldier than merely the ability to wield a sword.

In brief, we marched. We drilled. We practiced maneuvers, some of them quite sophisticated. I began to discover a healthy respect for the martial prowess of the Chac Yuul; they were as well-trained a body of fighting men as any I had ever encountered, on this world of Thanator or on my own Earth, and they were under an iron discipline that never faltered.

And I began to realize why the folk of Thanator

spoke of them in fear and trembling. They must have been the most splendid body of warriors on all this planet.

In the days that followed my entering the third cohort, I learned many tricks of warfare that I had never previously had reason to study.

For example, I mastered the technique of sword fighting while mounted on thaptor-back, which is a very different art from dueling on foot.

I became practised in the various tactics of using a Thanatorian weapon called the longspear, which, insofar as I know, is unique to the Thanatorians; at least, I have never heard of any such weapon ever being used by an earthly army. The longspear is just that, a long slender shaft of wood, measuring about twenty feet from heft to tip, ending in a steel claw or hook. The Thanatorian warriors use it on foot to dismount thaptormen in battle.

As well, Valkar and his lieutenants trained us in the use of the short throwing javelin which I had seen used ere this, in the lasso, a favorite weapon of the Thanatorians and in whose use they are amazingly adept, and with the hand axe and the war bow as well. I found myself tackling my meals with a ferocious appetite and slept each night the deep slumber of the bone-weary.

Valkar was an excellent officer: firm but restrained, utterly fair, and a man of his word. Each warrior under his command was given to know exactly what limits were set over his actions, beyond which he would stray at peril of punishment. The rules—which, incidentally, were original with Valkar himself, and were not the general orders obeyed throughout the rest of the Legion, as I later learned—were very precise. The women of the city were not to be molested, neither were the homes of the Shondakorians to be entered, on penalty of twenty lashes. Fighting with other warriors, drunkenness, and leaving the barracks during the night were punishable by ten lashes. To be caught sleeping on sentry duty was rewarded with death.

While most of my fellow warriors in the cohort of Valkar were an unruly lot, mere surly oafs for the most part, even the most brutish of them responded favorably to the just discipline of their commander. No man was ever punished on whim, and every man who was punished was made aware of the exact reasons for his culpability. Valkar explained that the Shondakorian citizens vastly outnumbered the occupying forces, and that while the presence of the Black Legion was tolerated, any abuse of the native women, or robbery of a native home, might well touch off the tinderbox and rouse the citizens to resistance. As well, he pointed out that a man who became drunk or who fell asleep on guard duty might well be responsible for the death of his comrades and the defeat of the Legion, were foes to creep past his post. The men came to reward Valkar with a grudging respect and, eventually, with a doglike devotion that was a testimonial to Valkar's ability to lead and to command.

Although Valkar and I were good friends, he gave me to understand that it would be detrimental to discipline were he to be seen to have a favorite among his own troops, hence I saw little of him in private during this early period of my service under his command. I, of course, understood the very good reasons for this, and my estimate of him grew. But we never met without a friendly word or look or smile and I was well aware that he kept a close eye on my progress. Indeed, ere long, once I had gained a certain proficiency in the martial arts, I was awarded a minor role in the training of the less intelligent and more awkward warriors, and from this I soon rose to the rank of squad leader, a rank equivalent to that of a second lieutenant.

As a minor officer, I had a semiprivate room near

the front of the barracks, which I shared with five or six other men of similar rank, and I ate in the officers' mess, in which Valkar himself dined. He found occasion to compliment me on my rise in the ranks, and we occasionally exchanged a friendly word.

Once my own training was over, and once the squadron under my command had completed their training in the finer arts of war, my duties slackened off. We were on duty one full day and off duty the next, which gave me frequent opportunities to explore the byways of the city and to discern something of its structure.

The fifteen men under my command were a brutal and oafish lot, but, bearing in mind the methods of command I had observed Valkar to use with such excellent results, I took to treating my men with utter fairness and utter firmness. I believe I won their respect quite early, when my authority was questioned and I was challenged by a hulking bully or two, whom I promptly and soundly whipped with the same sort of pugilistic display which had lowered Bluto in the dust. This small trial-by-combat was performed in privacy, and my superior officers never learned of it. If they had, the men I had fought and beaten would have been whipped until they were unconscious, a fact of which the men themselves were fully cognizant, and I believe they came to respect me all the more for the fact that I was willing to settle with them on my own without invoking the superior authority of the hierarchy of command.

At any rate, the general appearance and performance of my squadron was of an obviously superior degree, which earned us the commendation of our commander, and I found myself elevated to a full lieutenantcy and put in charge of two additional squadrons as well as my original command.

Weeks had passed, however, and I was nowhere nearer to finding the Princess Darloona than on the day I had entered the city.

I consoled myself grimly with the fact that at least I had a career in the military service if I desired it!

My new rank threw me quite often into close proximity with Valkar, for which I was grateful. For among the warriors of my command, or even among my fellow officers, I had found none of my own sort with whom to establish friendly intimacy. I think that Valkar, too, felt the loneliness of command, for his fellow *komors* were a brutal lot, given to gaming and drinking rather than to intelligent conversation. Hence he now rather frequently paid me the compliment of asking me to dine at his table, and not infrequently we went down into the city together on our off-duty days. I came to know him quite well, and, if anything, my respect and trust of him grew.

It was so obvious that he was of a finer sort than his fellow commanders, that I puzzled myself over the mystery of why a well-bred gentleman of good family such as he could have desired a place in the Chac Yuul, for by now I had learned that he had joined the Black Legion only a few months before my arrival. His rise through the ranks had been the mirror image of my own, for while the Chac Yuul are a band of coarse ruffians for the most part, the senior commanders of the host have a keen eye for a gifted and intelligent commander, be he of whatever race, and do not hesitate to promote such a man whenever they find one. But, all this notwithstanding, he seemed very out of place in their ranks, and more than once I mused curiously over the mystery he represented.

In all honesty, it never once occurred to me that his presence here might be accounted to much the same reason as that which had motivated my own.

The mystery deepened one evening some weeks after my rise to command. As our off-duty day had fallen on the same time, Valkar suggested we attend the theater together, and I readily agreed.

Dressed in our best, the medallions of our rank pinned to our leathern tunics, we found a box in a lower tier of the King Gamelion, a theater of supreme prominence in Shondakor; indeed, the Gamelion was virtually a national shrine of the arts, and its position was not unlike that of the Comédie Française in Paris, or the National Theatre of Great Britain. The highest families of Shondakor attend its performance of the national classics, and although most of the warrior nobility of the realm had fled into exile with Darloona and Lord Yarrak, her uncle, there were of course certain nobles or aristocrats unable to leave due to age, illness, or infirmity. Hence the cream of that which remained of Shondakorian society attended the Gamelion, as well as the upper crust of the Chac Yuul command, who were themselves now the dominant social class.

The play that night was unknown to me, a verse tragedy called *Parkand and Ylidore* by the renowned poet, Sorasto, of an earlier generation. My acquaintance with Thanatorian literature was rudimentary, hence I was all the more eager to repair that lack, and greeted Valkar's suggestion with enthusiasm.

I found the play an admirable work, not unlike some of the lesser dramas of Shakespeare, although the stilted dramatic vocabulary of an earlier epoch was somewhat difficult to follow.

Halfway during the first act, a stir went over the audience, and people turned to whisper to their companions, while casting a curious gaze at one of the boxes above. I turned to look, nudging Valkar, and froze with astonishment.

For there sat *Darloona*—my lost, loved Darloona!

She was pale but composed, and gorgeous in a gown of creamy lace with gems blazing at her throat. Accompanying her was a dark-faced, sardonic young man I had not seen before. He had a hard, mean look to his eyes, which were quick and cold and clever, and a thin-lipped mouth I did not like. His skin

had the swarthiness of a pure-bred Chac Yuul, but
his hair was sleek and black, inherited (I later
learned) from his mother, a Zanadarian. He wore the
most splendid uniform imaginable. It was a blaze of
glittering decorations and gilt.

I paled, gasped, and bit my lip, glancing at my
companion to see if he had noticed my sudden start.

To my utter amazement I saw that Valkar, too,
had paled, going white to the lips, and that a strange
emotion flamed in his grim cold eyes as he stared
aloft at the Princess and her unknown escort.

The mystery deepened! And it was soon to deepen
even more.

Busy with my thoughts, my mind a turmoil, I fear
I paid scant attention to the remainder of the drama
that evening, and to this hour I do not know whether
the Masked Prince disclosed his identity to the magi-
cian Zarakandus in time to prevent Ylidore from
marrying the wealthy merchant who had betrayed
her intimacy with the landless warrior to the choleric
baron into whose hands at all costs the mysterious
letter must be prevented from falling.

But I suspect my own inattention went unnoticed,
for Valkar himself seemed preoccupied with his own
thoughts that evening.

After the theater we repaired to a better-class wineshop in the neighborhood to share a bottle. And there
occurred an accident that only served to increase my
curiosity regarding my friend. For the mystery of his
background took a wholly new twist.

A serving girl by accident stumbled, spilling a gob-
let of wine on Valkar, splashing his face.

It was a trivial accident and he laughed aside the
girl's apologies, wiping the wine from his face with his
scarf.

The accident would have gone unnoticed, had it
not been for one small detail. I chanced to notice the
kerchief as Valkar replaced it within his tunic: a
smudge of dark tan substance discolored it.

Glancing at my friend, I noticed that the side of his face from which he had wiped the spilled wine now showed clear golden amber where before it had been dark tan.

A moment later, Valkar excused himself and left our booth to seek the sanitary facilities. Upon his return a moment later, the patch of clear golden skin was no longer evident.

I was intrigued, but kept my silence and made no comment, nor did I presume upon our friendship to pass a perhaps embarrassing question.

But I began to wonder why Valkar held a command in the Black Legion *in disguise!*

For he was no outcast half-breed as he had claimed.

The swarthy skin, which indicated Chac Yuul blood, and the black hair, which suggested Zanadarian parentage, had gone curiously with the emerald eyes of Shondakorian ancestry.

Now I suspected that beneath the false coloring of skin and hair, Valkar of Ganatol was a full-blooded Shondakorian.

But why the masquerade?

Who *was* Valkar?

BOOK TWO

THE BOOK OF VASPIAN

CHAPTER FIVE

I AM BEFRIENDED BY A PRINCE

Two days after I made the remarkable discovery that my friend Valkar was in reality a pure-bred Shondakorian in disguise, events took a new turn.

Strolling down one of the broad, tree-lined avenues of the Golden City of the Ku Thad, I heard cries of distress.

Gazing ahead, I perceived a chariot with a single passenger. The team of matched thaptors drawing the chariot were out of control, hurtling and careening down the boulevard at breakneck speed. At any instant, the chariot might overturn as its wheel caught an irregularity in the pave, thus hurling the chariot's occupant to the pave and dealing him a serious injury.

The thaptors might have stampeded from any one of a number of causes—a chance noise, a sudden movement, a flick of the whip on some tender portion of their anatomy, or sheer cantankerousness alone. For the weird bird-horses of Thanator have never been fully domesticated and are restive and unruly, and quite likely to bolt or to turn upon their rider on chance whim or the slightest provocation.

What I did was not a matter of conscious decision, or even of thought. It was purely instinctive. As the madly careening chariot approached the place where I stood, I sprang out into the street, full in its path, and waved my arms above my head with a sudden shout. I could have been trampled and maimed in the very next instant, but frankly the thought did not even occur to me.

The thaptor team came to a sudden halt and reared up in panic, slashing at empty air with their birdlike claws.

I leaped forward and seized their bridles and forced them down again. It was all over in an instant, but I must confess that I found myself shaking like a leaf, and drenched in cold perspiration from head to foot.

The lone passenger of the chariot sprang to the ground, pale and shaken as myself.

"My thanks, warrior," he gasped. "The Lords of Gordrimator alone know what made those empty-headed animals bolt like that. But had you not chanced along when you did, I might be a dead man at this moment!"

He wrung my hand in a grateful grip and I found myself staring in amazement at the lean, dark-faced, hard-eyed young man who had been Darloona's escort at the theater on that memorable evening!

Evidently he mistook my surprised expression for awe at his rank, for he smiled in a rather complacent manner. Frankly, I did not have even the slightest idea of who he was, for I had decided not to query Valkar on that point for fear of revealing my unusual interest in the Princess. But his next words disclosed the identity with which he naturally presumed me to be familiar.

"Yes, warrior, you have saved the life of your Prince!" he said. "And think not that the son of Arkola shall not remember and reward the heroic bravery of your deed. Your name and cohort?"

"Jandar, *kojat* of the third," I said rather dazedly. He nodded, smiled, accepted my salute, and vanished in the throng.

That evening as I returned to the barracks, I was told to report to the commander at once. I entered his office and saluted Valkar, who returned my salute absently, his gaze bent upon me and an expression of some perplexity visible in his features.

"Jandar, I was not aware that you were acquainted with Prince Vaspian," he remarked.

"Indeed, I am not," I replied. "To the best of my knowledge, I have only seen him twice; the first time at the theater the other night, and the second time was this morning, when I chanced to halt his runaway chariot by seizing the reins of the thaptors."

His brow cleared. "Ah, that explains the riddle! For I have received a note from the palace, commanding that you be detached from my command and assigned to the retinue of the Prince in recognition of your 'loyalty, bravery, self-sacrifice, and service to the crown.' It was this last that baffled me, as well it might."

I was elated at this opportunity to get inside the palace, but somewhat puzzled at the Prince's impulsive request.

"Do you mean to say that merely because I chanced along at just the right time to halt his runaways, I have been elevated to some sort of bodyguard of the Prince?" I asked.

He shook his head. "No, not just for that alone. Prince Vaspian inquired into your full record in the Black Legion, including a report on the way you handled that bully, Bluto, at the city gate, and your remarkable record in service, your rise to command, and so forth. He seems quite pleased with your career thus far."

"What sort of a person is this Prince?"

Valkar shrugged. "It is hard to say: I have had no personal contact with him, myself. But you must understand, Jandar, that the high councils of the Chac Yuul are ridden with rivalry and factionalism. The information that you are a veritable newcomer to the Legion seemed to delight His Highness most. You have no clan allegiances within the Black Legion, you see, and you have been with us for too brief a time to make very many close friends. Hence Prince Vaspian can trust in you to a considerable extent, where in another man he might fear a spy or even a carefully planted assassin. At any rate, he has fixed on you to join his retinue, and you are thus immediately detached from service to the third and reassigned to the palace. I shall be sorry to have you leave us."

This remarkable accident afforded me entrance into the palace and a chance to be near Darloona, hence I was tremendously excited by my good fortune. But I strove to conceal my elation, for I perceived that Valkar was somewhat saddened that we should see no more of each other and that our paths should part here.

"I shall regret leaving the cohort," I confessed, "and even more, I shall be sorry not to see you again. But perhaps my new assignment need not sever our friendship entirely, for surely we can continue to meet and to share our off-duty hours together, even as before."

He smiled, but shook his head reluctantly.

"I fear not, Jandar, for a mere *komor* has no business in the high circles of the Chac Yuul. But I shall not forget our friendship, and perhaps after all we shall meet again at a later time."

We bade each other farewell, and within the hour I was on the way to the palace compound with my few possessions bundled into the saddlebags of my thaptor.

At the very center of the city of Shondakor lies a square plaza, and on the northern side of this central plaza rises the ancient palace of the kings.

This palace has three main wings, and it is surrounded by parks and gardens which are themselves enclosed in a high wall, smaller, but no less strong and well guarded than the wall that encircles the vast metropolis itself. This inner enclosure forms the fortress citadel of the city and is designed to serve as the last defensive area in case the rest of the capital is

overwhelmed in siege. These things I had learned
from conversations with Lord Yarrak before setting
forth on my mission to rescue the Princess Darloona
from the stronghold of the Black Legion.

A pass, signed with the medallion of the Prince,
gave me entry into the palace enclosure, and a cham-
berlain led me through endless suites and corridors,
anterooms and apartments, meeting chambers and
feasting halls, to the north wing where the retinue of
Prince Vaspian was housed.

All about me lay scenes of vivid splendor and regal
luxury. No expense had been spared in decorating the
sumptuous apartments of the palace. Rare woods, ex-
quisite tapestries, precious gems and noble metals, had
been lavished on the ornamentation. Pierced lamps of
burnished silver shed an even glow over silken carpets
and carved ivory screens. Vases of sculptured jade,
amber, and gleaming onyx bore fresh-cut flowers.
Standing globes of perforated brass exuded coiling
threads of priceless incense to sweeten the air. Superb
statues of marble or bronze were enshrined in niches
along the high-roofed corridors. Gems flashed in the
folds of gorgeous tapestries. The masterworks of paint-
er, sculptor, and mosaicist adorned every room. The
luxury, the opulence, the beauty of the palace decor
was overwhelming. I recalled my brief tour of the citadel of Zanadar, months before, that time Lukor the
Swordmaster had smuggled me within the palace of
Prince Thuton in a last-moment effort to free our
Yathoon comrade, Koja, from death in the arena. Even
the kingly citadel of the City in the Clouds could not
outshine the sumptuous splendors of Shondakor.

Prince Vaspian met me in a glorious room whose
walls were hung with heavy folds of shining cloth.
The Prince was clothed in glistening white silks, diamonds flashing from lobe, brow, throat, wrist, and girdle. He acknowledged my salute with a casual wave
of a glittering hand and gestured for my attention.

"The servitors will take your belongings to your new

quarters," he said in a low voice. "I require your immediate services. In a short time I will attend a council meeting with my royal father and certain other lords of the Chac Yuul, here in this very chamber. I desire you to guard my person, for among the lords of the Legion are certain enemies who wish nothing so much as the chance to injure me. Do you understand?"

"I shall do whatever the Prince requires," I answered. "Precisely what are my instructions?"

He strode across the room and pointed to a low ottoman, one of a half circle of such.

"I will be seated here," he said. Then, striding behind the ottoman, he drew aside the curtains with a flourish, disclosing the yawning mouth of a black unlit passage.

"You will station yourself here," he said. "All you have to do is keep your eyes open and watch for treachery. If anyone makes a move towards me, strike to defend my person. Here you will be unseen, for the curtains are opaque unless one stands very close to their folds, in which case the fabric can be seen to be transparent. Remain completely silent, regardless of what may happen—and do not let anyone know you are there unless there is an attempt upon my life. Is this clear?"

"Perfectly," I nodded. "And what do I do later on?"

"At the conclusion of the council, we will all file out. It would not be wise for you to emerge from your hiding place in order to accompany me, for that would give away the fact that I suspect treason and am guarding myself accordingly. Therefore, once all have left the chamber, you may withdraw. At the end of this passage you will find a secret door which leads out into a corridor. Go out into the open and ask directions of whomever you should meet. Go at once to my suite and my servitors will show you to the room set aside for yourself; remain there until I call for you.

My servitors will bring you wine or food or whatever else you may require. You may sleep, if you like."

"I understand," I said.

"Very good. Now take your position behind the curtains, and be careful not to give away your presence by a word or a sound!"

I stepped through the shining curtains to stand in the unlit doorway of the secret passage. Standing close to the curtains I saw that it was indeed easy to see through them, for at intervals in the heavier weave, gauze-thin patches of a lighter fabric of identical hue were set, as if for this very purpose.

Vaspian withdrew swiftly from the room and I settled down to await whatever should happen.

After a few minutes, several Chac Yuul guards filed into the room and took up positions on either side of the door, holding long spears, the light from bright-paned windows sparkling off their helmets of burnished copper adorned with small cubes of silver.

Then several men entered, one by one. They were squat, burly, and heavy-thewed, obviously warriors, although no longer young men. Probably high-ranking officers of the Black Legion. They had a swaggering, piratical look about them—men accustomed to power, command, authority—men who had led the bandit legion in many battles, sieges, and forays.

Next followed my "patron," Prince Vaspian, a haughty look on his dark, lean, and not-unhandsome face. He disdained to notice the courteous manner in which the senior officers of the Legion rose to salute him. He stalked across the room to the low ottoman he had indicated to me earlier, and seated himself directly in front of the place where I was standing.

No sooner had he taken his seat than another individual entered, and the Prince struggled reluctantly to his feet again to stand in the presence of Arkola the Usurper himself, the all-powerful Warlord of the Black Legion.

He was a remarkable personage: a most impressive

man; the almost tangible aura of supreme power radiated from his powerful frame and heavyset features. Of course, he was no stranger to me, for I had seen him once before, or his image, mirrored in the *palungordra** I had seen in operation weeks before, in Zanadar, at which time I had overheard a conversation between Arkola and Prince Thuton of the Sky Pirates from a concealed passageway in the walls of the royal citadel.

The face of the Usurper was powerfully molded, with a square jaw and a heavy, scowling brow. His thick neck was sunk between burly shoulders, and his long, massive arms and deep chest were banded with thick sinews like heavy cables. He was no bandy-legged dwarf, like so many of the Chac Yuul, but a veritable Hercules of a man, no taller than myself, but much heavier and stronger.

His features—coarse, blunt, brutal—caught and held your attention. He had a swarthy complexion and a bullet-head covered with lank colorless hair of a peculiar consistency, unlike his son's black hair. Gold baubles flashed in his earlobes and a chain of fire-rubies smoldered about his thickly corded neck. Under scowling black brows, his eyes were fierce yellow pits of somber, lion-like flame. This was no man to trifle with. This was a man born to command others. He wore simple warrior's leather—the familiar high-necked tunic worn all over Thanator—open at the throat and displaying a thatch of body fur and the curve of heavy pectoral muscles. Emblazoned on the breast of his tunic was the dread emblem of the Black Legion, a black horned and fanged grinning skull with eyes of scarlet flame.

Flung loosely about his massive shoulders were

---

* These ingenious television crystals are among the more amazing instruments perfected by Thanatorian science. The term translates as "the far-seeing eyes," and the incident to which Captain Dark alludes may be found in the first volume of these adventures, *Jandar of Callisto*, Chapter 11.—L.C.

magnificent robes of emerald and saffron velvet, heavily embroidered with stiff gold wire, falling to swish around his booted ankles.

Amid utter silence the Lord of the Black Legion took his place at the center of the half circle of ottomans, on a dais slightly raised above the level of the rest. His son, the Prince Vaspian, sat on his left hand. The ottoman to his right was unoccupied.

Now there entered into the chamber the last member of the high council of the Chac Yuul.

I had heard of him, but had never seen him before. Nevertheless, I recognized him the instant he entered the room. Ool the Uncanny, they called him, and among the conquering lords of the Black Legion he was a power to be reckoned with.

A fat, placid-faced little man in gray robes, his hands muffled in the long sleeves, came shuffling into the council chamber. A certain stillness came over the other occupants of the room.

The little man was bald as an egg, his face butter-yellow, his slitted eyes black and cold as frozen ink. A gentle smile hovered perpetually on his features. He looked as peaceful and harmless as a man could look. Why, then, did my nape hairs stiffen and a prickle of awe roughen the surface of my skin?

From the awkward silence of the others, I knew that my own almost instinctive loathing and fear of the harmless-looking little fat man was shared by them as well. About him, it seemed, blew a cold, ghastly wind from the hidden places of nature. The chill, dank breath of the Unknown . . . an icy, nameless wind from the dark abyss of the Ultimate Pit. . . .

Who he was, this little man who called himself Ool, and from whence he had come, was cloaked in mystery. No man knew his heart, and only the shadow gods he worshipped knew the secret recesses of his soul.

Some men called him wizard; others called him priest; and there were yet others, and they were not few in number, who called him a black-hearted devil in mortal flesh.

Such a being was Ool the Uncanny, warlock of the Chac Yuul, priest of the Dark Powers, servant of the Unknown.

CHAPTER SIX

THE SECRET COUNCIL

Now that the seven lords of the Black Legion were assembled, the council began.

Arkola spoke in a deep, strong voice.

"Lords, you have all seen the ultimatum delivered by the messenger of the Zanadarians, and you are all familiar with our present position. What say you to the threats of Prince Thuton?"

One of the senior commanders, a grizzled, scar-faced old warrior, growled: "I say let us cast his insolent demands back in his teeth!"

One or two of the other commanders added guttural agreements to this, position. Arkola cleared his throat and silence fell.

"True enough. After all, when have the warriors of the Chac Yuul shrunk from war? Yet consider: the flying contraptions of Zanadar are powerful weapons. We have no defense against attack from the skies, for all the power our fighting men display on the land."

My patron, Prince Vaspian, spoke up, silkily.

"Surely, my father, you do not intend paying the price I had almost said, the tribute—demanded by this affrontive Lord of the Sky Pirates?"

Arkola's scowl deepened.

"Someday, if he lives long enough, it may be that the Prince, my son, will learn that gold may be given away without loss or harm to a man, and that more gold may be gotten to replace it. Whereas a man's life, once he has parted with it, cannot be replaced. What is a few thousand pieces of gold to us? We shall wring

many times that sum from the fat-gutted merchants of
Shondakor before the year is out. And, I say again, we
have no defense against the flying machines of the
City in the Clouds!"

"All this is true, Arkola, but never yet has any foe
forced the Black Legion to pay tribute to escape from
the danger of battle," growled the grizzled old warrior
who had spoken up before—his name, I later learned,
was Murrak. "How will the men take it? What will it
do to their morale, and to the degree of confidence
they place in us, their commanders? And will not the
payment of one tribute without quarrel but spur this
wily Thuton to demand yet further tribute at a later
date? Perhaps we should take a firm stand now; and
fight it we must, for later, when we are wrung dry, we
shall have to fight after all!"

Arkola permitted his grim face to relax in a grin.

"Now, those are wise, shrewd arguments, and there
is much good sense behind them," he nodded. "If the
Prince, my son, had but half the wits of my lord commanders of the Legion, he would make his father proud
of him. Alas, I fear the hand of a woman has softened
his manhood and beclouded his mind."

A chuckle ran around the semicircle and the dark
face of Prince Vaspian flushed angrily, but he wisely
refrained from making a reply. I began to get the notion that the "enemy" Vaspian fancied he had among
the council was his own father.

Flushed, sullen, Prince Vaspian made no reply. His
father smiled, a cold hard smile.

"And since the root and cause of our present dilemma is that same love which has somewhat softened his manly strength, it behooves my son to think
twice ere he impute the warriors of the Black Legion
and slander their honor. Know that if we do indeed
make payment, as demanded, it will not be 'tribute'
but a calculated investment which will buy us valuable time."

Then one of the warrior lords, a balding but burly-shouldered old commander spoke up, and his words froze me with a shock of unbelieving astonishment.

"Since my lord has already raised the matter, may I ask when we shall celebrate the nuptials of the Prince Vaspian and the Lady Darloona?" he asked.

I started involuntarily. For a moment I could hardly believe my ears. Darloona and this puny Prince? It did not seem possible. I strained my every sense, following the conversation.

"The Princess demands that it be very soon," Vaspian said, and he smirked a trifle as he said it, and at the suggestion of a sniggering leer in his tones I could cheerfully have strangled him on the spot.

Arkola snorted. "Never shall I understand how the Prince my son has managed to win the affections of so strong-willed and womanly a bride-to-be," he said with a mocking half-smile. "However, this marriage will give the seal of legitimacy to our possession of the throne, and I oppose it not."

"She is mad with love for me," the Prince said loudly, almost boastingly. "Every day that passes seems to her an unendurable delay!"

"Ah? Well, let us pass to more significant matters," Arkola said.

Turning from the boastful Prince, Arkola directed his attentions to the one member of this council who had yet to speak. The little wizard-priest, Ool, had sat quietly through all this, plump soft hands folded in the deep sleeves of his robe, his bald, buttery face placid and unreadable. Like a cold, malignant little Buddha he squatted, clever slitted eyes roving from face to face, listening to every word, but never permitting the slightest shadow of a reaction to mar the calm indifference of his impenetrable serenity.

"What says the Uncanny One to these dangers that now confront us?" demanded Arkola. The little priest put his head on one side, considering. Then he spoke, and his voice was mild and gentle, soft and high of pitch.

"Like all mighty men of valor, my lord, you reduce the range of possible actions to the simple alternatives of battle or surrender. However, there remain other avenues open to us."

"And what are they?" Arkola growled. "I confess I can see no other choice but to either pay the price the Zanadarians ask, or refuse to pay it and face a battle."

The priest nodded, candlelight glistening on his round bald pate.

"Yet other solutions do exist," he said mildly. "Let me call them to your attention, and to the attention of my lords. Suppose—" a sweet smile hovered about his lips and benevolence beamed in his cherubic expression "—suppose we refuse to acknowledge our debt, and yet Thuton is *unable* to attack us."

Murrak, the grizzled old war leader, stared at the calm little priest in puzzlement.

"How 'unable'?" he rumbled.

"From illness, perchance," Ool purred, his face placid and his voice gentle. "There are ways, you know, my lords! A letter from this council to his hands—a letter imbued with a toxic venom—or a gift of nubile female slaves, each infected with a virulent fever—or a jeweled gaud, some precious bauble, with a sharp edge calculated to cut his fingers, an edge steeped in some poisonous decoction. . . ."

I have heard the voice of evil in my time, but I must confess that my blood ran cold as I listened to the soft, mild voice of this smiling little priest as he discussed the ways and means of poisoning a man without his knowledge. And I consider it much to the credit of the lords of the Black Legion, simple, hard, practical war veterans all, and no subtle Borgias, that they were almost as revolted as I at the oily, purring suggestions proffered by Ool the Uncanny.

"My Lord!" Murrak appealed to Arkola. "Never would a Black Legion warrior sully his honor by stooping to such vileness! Surely, you cannot consider —will not consider—"

Arkola pondered the priest's words, jaw resting on one scarred fist, his cold eyes thoughtful. I could see his mind exploring, however reluctantly, the possible avenues of action opened up by such a plan. But his grim mouth was puckered with distaste and sour disapproval was stamped into his features.

His reply temporized without actually giving a firm answer to the little priest's proposal. Then the conversation turned to a more general discussion of fighting strength and military preparations. I gathered from the following converse that Prince Thuton of the Sky Pirates demanded payment for the person of Darloona. Some while before she had been captured by the Chac Yuul, Darloona had been a guest or prisoner of the Zanadarian monarch; our escape from the City in the Clouds had been occasioned by my chance discovery that the treacherous Thuton, while pretending to espouse her cause, had actually been negotiating secretly with Arkola over her person. He had demanded a heavy price for her, but had been willing to sell the Princess of Shondakor to her enemies.

Now that her escape from Zanadar had brought her so swiftly into the clutches of the Chac Yuul, Thuton evidently believed that Arkola had somehow had a hand in that escape—which was completely untrue. But it seemed he now demanded full payment of the ransom, on the threat of all-out war. This was the dilemma in which the conquering legions of Arkola now found themselves.

Little of the conversation that ensued registered on my mind. My brain was a whirling turmoil of consternation, caused by the incredible discovery that the woman I loved would soon wed the sly, foppish Prince of the Black Legion—*and by her own desire,* or so it was given out. I could not and would not believe this terrible news to be true. Doubtless a helpless prisoner of the Prince, Darloona was being forced into this wedding.

Whatever the true reason for her acceptance of
Vaspian's proposal, I must know it. I must hear from
her own lips that she truly desired to wed the Black
Legion Prince, or I would never believe it.

A thousand thoughts went through my dazed mind.
That I loved the proud and beautiful Princess with
every atom of manhood in my body, mind, and soul,
was known only to me. She knew nothing of my love,
for never had I dared to speak of it—indeed, the full
realization of my love had only burst upon me when
she had been taken from my side, and hence the opportunity to speak of it had never arisen.

I know not what she thought of me. Surely, by
now, her first contempt had been allayed. Through a
series of confusions and accidents, Darloona had become persuaded that I was a coward and an honorless
weakling. My labors in her behalf, my striving to rescue her from the grip of her wily and treacherous
enemy, Thuton, must have proved to her that her
original opinions of me were inaccurate. At any rate,
I must hear the truth from her own lips.

And I dreaded the moment when I should learn the
truth!

Not long after this, the Black Legion council broke
up and the lords departed their several ways. My patron, Prince Vaspian, rose languidly to his feet, drawing about his slender shoulders a hooded cloak of dark
green velvet, and left the chamber after directing a
secret glance of dismissal at the hidden position where
I stood, concealed from all eyes by the draperies.

In obedience to his command, I retreated from the
opening and made my own exit from the chamber by
means of the secret passageway whose presence he
had indicated to me.

This passage, I noted, connected with yet others.
The walls of the royal palace of Shondakor were thick,
and it seemed they contained a maze of secret tunnels

and sliding panels and spyholes even as had the mighty citadel of Zanadar.

Whim directed me to explore these passageways a bit before going to my quarters in the Prince's suite. I had no way of knowing but what a working knowledge of this secret network of hidden passages might someday soon become valuable to me.

The walls of the tunnels were at intervals pierced with spyholes. Small shields masked these eyeholes. Sliding them aside I saw that the passageways had carried me deep within the royal precincts of the palace.

I vowed to explore just a bit farther before turning back and going about my business.

The sound of muffled voices conversing in low tones drew me to one particular eyehole. I slid the shield aside, set my eye to the tiny aperture, and found myself gazing into a sumptuously appointed apartment. From the delicacy and luxuriousness of the decorations, I assumed it was a lady's boudoir.

I had but slender opportunity to observe the decor, however, as my attention was seized by the two figures who stood within the center of the room. They were a man and a woman, but I could not see their faces and from the faint murmur of their voices I could not even make out what they were saying to each other, except that the woman seemed to be pleading tenderly and the man giving quiet refusal.

With a shock of amazement I saw that the man was none other than my princely patron, Vaspian himself!

Or—as his back was turned to me and I could see nothing of his features—I assumed that the figure was that of Prince Vaspian. At least he wore a green cowled cloak like the one I had observed the son of Arkola to don before leaving the council chamber some little while before.

And now as he embraced the woman passionately, his hood fell back as the movement of his arms dislodged it, and I saw that he had the same sleek, black hair as the Prince.

And the next moment I made a discovery that drove the breath from my body in a gasp of astonishment . . . a discovery which plunged my spirits into profound depression . . . a discovery at which I turned silently away with averted face and bowed shoulders, and left the maze of secret tunnels for the quiet of my room.

For in the intensity of their emotions, the man swung the woman he was embracing about so that from my secret hiding place I could see her features perfectly.

That rippling glory of red-gold hair—that tawny amber skin—that full, ripe, passionate mouth and those slanted, glorious eyes of deep emerald mystery—there could be no mistake.

It was Darloona of Shondakor, the woman I loved!

Darloona, clasped in a close embrace, her tear-wet cheeks and quivering ripe lips giving clear evidence of the intensity of her emotion, with—*Prince Vaspian!*

CHAPTER SEVEN

MARUD'S MISSION

The apartments that formed the suite of Prince Vaspian were superb. Glistening floors of marble tile, walls of fretted stone hung with beautiful old tapestries, lit by hanging lamps of pierced silver. There were, surprisingly, very few servants. I suppose this reflected the all but neurotic suspicions the Prince held towards nearly everyone around him. There were few that he felt he could trust, least of all, his servants.

The apartments were in a far corner of one wing of the royal palace, quite secluded and separated by many rooms from the main corridors. I was given a small but comfortably furnished room situated between the Prince's living quarters and the main palace. I suppose that Vaspian figured any foes or spies or assassins dispatched by his enemies would have to manage to get past me before they could do him whatever harm they contemplated. The whole situation would have been rather amusing if it had not been so depressing.

During my first few days as chief bodyguard in the retinue of the Prince I had little enough to do. The Chac Yuul were still, in many ways, an occupying force—a conquering horde, holding the territories they had seized and momentarily expecting to have to do battle for them. Hence there was little in the way of court functions, balls, or masquerades. Arkola held court each day towards the hour of noon, signing proclamations, judging disputes, settling quarrels. The afternoon he spent training with his warriors or reviewing them.

Prince Vaspian had little interest in either of these matters. He was a very spoiled young man, vain and suspicious, idle and without any particular interests that I could see. He was certainly no warrior, hence mingling with the Black Legion soldiers was distasteful to him. Nor did he seem interested in the internal administration of the Legion and kept well away from his father's court of justice. It was the shadowy subworld of plot and counterplot, political maneuvering and rivalry, that consumed him. Those of the lords of the Black Legion that I had observed thus far were, with the single exception of Ool the Uncanny, and perhaps with the exception of the Usurper himself, simple war leaders, hard, strong men of camp and field, totally disinterested in the court intrigues of the Byzantine variety favored by Prince Vaspian. I have no doubt that Murrak and the other war leaders disliked Vaspian, for he was not at all their sort, and his sharp tongue, furtive eyes, and clever words would earn him few friends in any circle. But I could hardly conceive that they were plotting against him. For the most part, they simply left him alone.

As for Arkola, he seemed alternately amused and disgusted by his son. He seemed an able administrator and a powerful leader of men, with enormous charisma and an almost total lack of scruples. The oily intrigues, the cunning hints, the psychotic aura of suspicion and deceit and fear and envy that hung constantly about his son roused him to contempt.

While Vaspian seldom showed himself at what few court functions there were, he insisted on my being present. I was supposed to report back to him the words and actions of his "enemies." And thus I suffered through endless tribal disputes, property settlements, arguments over new laws, and the like. Upon my return to the Prince's quarters each day I was endlessly questioned about every conceivable detail of

what had taken place. In what tone of voice had this
or that *komor* argued for his clan? To whom did this
or that lord glance when a certain question was
raised? Had I seen this captain of the Chac Yuul whispering to that captain? Were any notes passed at the
tribal court? Endless, reiterative, and boring were
these sessions with the Prince my patron; and were it
not for the fact that my service in his retinue had
gained me entrance into the palace where Darloona
was held, I cannot but think I should long since have
somehow severed relations.

As for Darloona, I hardly ever saw her, and never
close enough to speak to or even close enough for her
to see me. A couple of times she appeared at the evening banquet, usually on the Prince's arm, and since
I was stationed immediately behind the cushioned
seat where Vaspian sat at table, the first time she
made her appearance I was seized with fear that she
would recognize me. But it seems that it is not the custom of the Chac Yuul to mingle with their women at
table, and hence she was seated some distance from
the lords of the Black Legion.

I devoured her with my eyes, being careful to cast
my own gaze downwards whenever she chanced to
look my way.

But the eyes of the Princess invariably passed over
me without lingering for a single moment or displaying the slightest flicker of either interest or recognition.

But it seems that my surreptitious gaze had caught
the attention of at least one of the Lords of the Black
Legion.

For, turning my eyes from Darloona, I found the
cold, slitted gaze of Ool the Uncanny fixed upon me
with speculative curiosity. A slight smile hovered over
the placid features of the little wizard-priest, and I
turned my eyes away with a semblance of indifference, trying to convey the impression that my attention to the Princess had merely been curiosity or some

other idle emotion, and that I had not really noticed that my actions were under the scrutiny of Ool.

During my tenure in the ranks of the Black Legion I had set about to learn something of its recent history.

I had heard a few puzzling and cryptic hints as to the mode whereby the Chac Yuul had taken the walled city of Shondakor on the banks of the river Ajand. It was a bit curious that the city should have fallen so swiftly and so easily to its enemies. Generally, a city so walled about with strong masonry and so closely guarded, as from its gates and portcullises and barbicans and guard towers Shondakor seemed to have been, would have been able to stand against a siege for a very considerable length of time. I had heard, ere now, some reference to the fact that Shondakor had fallen virtually without siege—that the Black Legion warriors had been within the walls in force even before the first alarm was given.

I became friendly with some officers of my own rank who were also attached to palace duty, although I was careful not to form any relationship with a member of the retinue of any of the other lords, for fear of arousing the suspicions of my patron. Plying them with liquor on our off-duty hours, I learned much of the conquest of Shondakor.

Rather than bore my reader with a lengthy account of these conversations, I shall give the gist of what I gleaned from hours of desultory talk.

It seems that there was a secret entrance into the city known to but a few. Shondakor was very ancient and many kings had held sway over the Golden City of the Ku Thad. During the long-ago days of some remote dynasty, a hidden entrance had been built whereby the main gates could be circumvented. Even the present royal house was not in possession of this secret, but the arts of Ool the Uncanny had, it seemed, discovered the whereabouts of the hidden door and by its means the Black Legion had gained entry into the city in numbers sufficient to take it before an adequate defense could be mounted.

As my reader can imagine, this news I found most exciting. If such a route could be made known to the Ku Thad force hiding in the jungles of the Grand Kumala, they might make very good use of this information to retake the city themselves. It would indeed be ironic if the secret entrance which had permitted the Black Legion to gain entry into Shondakor were to prove the very method of their undoing.

The secret entrance was not exactly a secret after all, as many hundreds of the Chac Yuul had gone through it before the gates were seized and the main body of the Legion entered the city.

Ere long I found one of the squat little warriors who had been among the advance guard into the city, and luckily he had a weakness for a certain strong liquor called *quarra*. From him I learned that the hidden route was not a secret gate in the walls, but a passageway tunneled beneath the walls and beneath the river itself! An astounding engineering feat, to be sure; and now that I knew the secret it was vital that I somehow pass it along to Lord Yarrak and his warriors. But I could hardly ride out of the city and into the jungles without arousing the suspicions of the Chac Yuul.

Fortunately, before parting from Lord Yarrak, he had envisioned the possibility that I should require a method of communication with him, and he had given me the name of a certain innkeeper in Shondakor who was friendly to the royal cause and who acted in the capacity of a secret agent, smuggling out information to the Ku Thad whenever it became needful to do so.

On one of my off-duty hours I found occasion to enter this inn, which was called The Nine Flagons, and drawing the innkeeper aside I exchanged with

him the secret password which Yarrak had taught me.
I entrusted to him a letter to Lord Yarrak wherein I
divulged the hidden entrance to the tunnel. In that
letter I also counseled Lord Yarrak to be patient and
not to use the secret tunnel until such time as I gave
the word, for I had yet to arrange with the Princess
our escape.

The innkeeper, a large, red-faced man named
Marud, promised to convey the message that very
night.

"Gods, Captain," he wheezed, for Vaspian had elevated me to the rank of *komad* upon entering his service. "I have kept my eyes and ears open for months,
strivin' to learn how these bandy-legged little horebs
whelmed the city so sudden-like, and naught did I
get for all my pains. You should only know how much
free wine I ha' poured down Chac Yuul gullets trying
to loosen a few tongues!" He chuckled, his vast paunch
quivering with seismic ripples of humor.

"They be a close-mouthed lot, yet you ha' pried
some valuable matters out," he said.

"You will have no difficulty in getting through the
secret tunnel, will you?" I asked. "I have not been
able to discover if it is guarded or not, but if it is, at
least no guards are stationed out in the open."

He winked, grinning with irrepressible humor.

"Never you mind your heart about *that*, Captain!
Old Marud has a trick er two in his old head. You
just get along back to your place in th' palace, and
leave the rest of it to me. I'll get yer letter into the
hands of my Lord Yarrak, never you fear!"

And wiping his red hands on a filthy apron, the
bald, fat little old innkeeper went waddling off to
tend to the needs of his customers. I stood and
watched him go with a bemused eye.

Vast of paunch, red of face, short of breath, the
wheezing old fellow certainly did not have about him
the air of a hero—he looked more the buffoon, if any-

thing. But this very night would try his qualities to the utmost, and we should see if he had the stuff of heroes in him.

Rarely has so much ridden upon the shoulders of a single man.

Darloona's fate, and my own, and that of all Shondakor, lay in that letter old Marud had so carelessly stuffed into his leathern girdle. Well . . . we should see what happened. . . .

I returned to the palace without incident and made my way to the remote corner of that wing wherein the Prince's suite of rooms was found. I disrobed and sought my pallet, but sleep did not come to me for a long time. For I was baffled by this priest they called Ool the Uncanny, and I marveled that he, an outsider, should have known of the secret tunnel under the walls of Shondakor when even the ruling dynasty of the city knew it not. (For had they known it existed, surely they would have had it guarded heavily or sealed up.)

What strange powers did this little man possess? And what role was he to play in this adventure?

At length, despite the tension and turmoil in my mind, the urge to sleep overcame me and I slumbered.

The skies of Thanator, those strange, shifting skies of golden vapor, lit suddenly with the sourceless glory of the dawn.

I became aware of running feet thudding down the corridor beyond my chamber. The shouts of distant voices came to me, and there was urgency in them although I could not make out any words. On sudden impulse I rose, drew on my leathern tunic, slung the baldric, scabbard, and sword about my shoulders, laced on my buskins, and went out to learn, if I could, the nature of this unwarranted excitement.

I intercepted a guard captain whom I knew slightly.

"What is all the disturbance, Narga? Is the palace being attacked?" I asked, laying my hand on his shoulder as he hurried by me.

"No, Jandar, nothing like that. But they have taken a spy!" he said curtly.

"Who has?"

"They who serve the Lord Ool," was his rejoinder. "The spy was attempting to use the secret passage under the river and the walls, but was seized by the guards which the Lord Ool had commanded to be posted at that place."

The chill breath of presentiment was blowing upon my nape.

"Is the name of the spy known?" I asked, with whatever semblance of casualness I could summon.

He nodded. "It is one Marud, a fat innkeeper of the city," he grunted. "It seems he was attempting to convey some sort of message to the rebels in the jungle, but the Uncanny One, with his shadowy arts, gained forewarning of the plot."

"I see," I said, and I fear my face went pale at this dire news, although so dim was the illumination at this hour that I doubt if my acquaintance noticed.

"Was he taken with the message on him?" I asked.

"No; or so I have been told. They seized him and carried him before Arkola the Warlord, but . . . ."

"But?"

"But he snatched a dagger from one of the guards escorting him and slew himself before he could be questioned," he said. And then, saying he was called to his post, he bid me good-day and went on down the corridor, leaving me to my thoughts.

Alas, brave, loyal Marud! Obviously, he had slain himself rather than betray my part in this business. I felt a qualm of conscience. A man had killed himself to save me. Or, rather, to save me that I might yet serve the Princess Darloona.

Well, he was not the first patriot to die in the service of a worthy cause, and he would not be the last. But

I determined then and there that, once this dire business was resolved, and all our present dangers at an end, Marud's sacrifice should not be forgotten nor his name go unremembered.

But one overwhelming question soon filled my mind to the exclusion of all other matters. Had Marud been seized *before* delivering my letter to Lord Yarrak—or *after* doing so?

During that morning I made inquiry as best I could, but none could answer me this riddle. Marud had been arrested in the entrance to the tunnel, but he could either have been about to leave the city or about to re-enter it at the time he was seized. And no one knew which!

Unless it was Ool the Uncanny!

CHAPTER EIGHT

OOL THE UNCANNY

For the next couple of days I walked cautiously, expecting at almost any time to be arrested. But nothing of that nature came to pass, nor was I under surveillance, so far as I could judge, or even under suspicion. Gradually, I relaxed, thinking myself safe and my role in the unfortunate martyrdom of Marud unknown.

My patron had dispatched me on an errand of small importance, which took me into a portion of the palace I had never visited till now.

Delivering his message, I was on my way back to Prince Vaspian's apartments when suddenly a soft voice from behind me halted me in my tracks.

I turned to look into the cold, glinting eyes of Ool the Uncanny!

The fat little man smiled at the involuntary expression of surprise that must have shown on my features.

"Ah, it is the *komad* Jandar," he purred in his silky voice. "We have not yet had the opportunity to meet, *komad*, although I have followed your rise in the ranks with considerable interest."

"I am surprised that the Lord Ool has any interest at all in a mere warrior such as myself," I said. He laughed in a most peculiar way without making a sound.

"Ah, but I am interested in everything which touches upon the safety of my Lord Prince Vaspian," he said. "Come—you have a moment, surely—there is chilled wine in my quarters here—indulge me for a moment."

I accepted his invitation after some little hesitation. I was in no way afraid of this fat, buttery little priest, and I was very curious to know more about him. So I permitted him to usher me into a large chamber where he evidently dwelt.

It was a spacious, sunny room, very comfortably furnished, with thick carpets and gorgeous wall hangings and cushioned chairs. He poured me an excellent yellow wine in frosted goblets of silver and set beside me a platter of small pastries and cold sliced meats. I observed to myself that this priest obviously did not live in stark poverty but liked his bodily comforts.

I also resolved not to sample aught of food and drink in his presence, lest it be embued with some narcotic of a tongue-loosening nature. So I but moistened my lips with the wine and politely refused the pastries, saying I had just eaten, which was true enough.

Ool seated himself across from me and folded his plump soft hands across his belly, regarding me with cunning, observant eyes and a slight smile which did nothing to warm the coldness of his reptilian gaze. And I became aware that he had seated me so that I faced the windows and my face was clearly illuminated, while he himself had his back to them and was in shadow.

"Now, then, *komad,* we can gossip for a breath in comfort. . . . I believe you were last in service to the Lord of Soraba?"

I replied that this was true.

"And was my Lord Kaamurath still regnant in that city when you were there?" he inquired, which rather surprised me, for when we had chosen Soraba to be my fictitious last place of mercenary service we did so on the knowledge that the Black Legion had been far distant from that city on the shores of the Corund Laj for years, and hence there was little likelihood of my having to answer any embarrassing questions about a city which I had never seen in my life.

"Why, yes," I replied, "although somewhat aged."

This was true, or so Lord Yarrak had assured me. For he had carefully primed me with certain items of information about Soraba in case I *did* have to answer any queries about my service in that city.

Ool nodded thoughtfully, and then inquired after the health of someone called Lord Urush. I had never heard of this personage, and decided to temporize. So I laughed and said that I had been a mere swordsman in the city guard and had come into only the smallest contact with the great lords.

Ool's smile deepened. I did not like the way he smiled. Nor the cold glitter of his black eyes as they peered cunningly at me.

"Naturally, that would be so," he purred. "Yet is it not odd that with only a few weeks service here in Shondakor you have risen to a high rank and a place beside the Prince Vaspian himself, while for all the length of your service in Soraba you remained a mere swordsman?"

I shrugged with seeming casualness, although perspiration was running down my ribs under my leather tunic.

"No, not odd at all, my lord. My commander in Soraba was a self-seeking man who sought to curry favor with the great houses of that city by promoting only their younger sons, and passing over deserving but less well-attached warriors like myself. And as you must know, my lord, it was not my military honors which attracted the favor of my Lord Prince Vaspian to elevate me to his retinue, but a lucky chance whereby I was able to rescue him from danger by halting a runaway thaptor."

"Ah, yes, somewhat of that story I have heard ere now—a most fortunate accident indeed, as the Prince was unharmed by it, and as you rose to good fortune by this same accident. From what land do you hail, *komad*? Never have I met a man with eyes and hair the color of yours."

"A country called the United States of America," I replied.

"What an odd name! I do not believe that I have ever heard of that city. Where is it?" he inquired lazily, and still that smile hovered about his full lips.

I felt that I was being played with, but there was nothing that I could do about it. Now I knew what it was like to be a small mouse at the pleasure of a smiling, lazy, fat, and very well-fed cat.

"It lies a very great distance from these parts," I said, and truthfully enough. "I am uncertain of the direction, for I have been long from my homeland and have visited many lands since leaving it."

"It must indeed be very distant," Ool said lazily, "for I have never heard of it, and geography has long been a hobby of mine. Tell me, *komad*, do all of your fellow citizens in that land have eyes of such a rare color?"

"No, not all. We are a nation made up of several peoples who have long interbred. A considerable number of my fellow countrymen have blue eyes, however. They seem to be the most rare here."

"Indeed they are, most rare, most rare indeed!" he said, and once again he gave that soundless laugh which made my skin crawl, although for the life of me, I could not say why. But there was something about this fat, soft, mild-seeming little wizard-priest that instinctively put me on the alert. I had the feeling that he was about as harmless as a cobra.

I brought the interview to a close at this point, pleading that I dared not be too long absent from the side of my patron.

"Ah, yes, the Lord Prince is somewhat, shall we say —oversuspicious?" he purred, rubbing his fat little hands together. "He has the strange feeling that he is surrounded by unfriendly persons with great secrets —an odd thing to fear, is it not? Tell me, *komad*, have you secrets which you hold to yourself?"

I forced an awkward laugh. "Of course, my lord!

Does not every man have a secret or two?"

He laughed again, rising to usher me out of his silken little nest.

"Oh, yes—but some of us have the most astounding secrets!" he chuckled, and I did not like the sound of that remark at all.

I bowed my farewell and made my way off down the corridor. And all the way I felt his cold, glittering little eyes on me until I had turned the corner and was out of sight.

And thus concluded my private interview with Ool the Uncanny. I had the feeling that he either knew or suspected that there was something about me which I did not wish known. But he did not thereafter interfere with my actions nor make any report of me to those who were my superiors, so I could not be certain.

But thereafter I avoided him as best I could. And, luckily, Prince Vaspian did not again send me into that portion of the royal palace.

The following evening and for several nights thereafter I attended my patron at these court feasts I have ere now spoken of, so I had frequently the opportunity of seeing Darloona and of observing her in public.

Ool the Uncanny was often present on these occasions, so I was careful not to let myself seem overly interested in the Princess. I felt he was already suspicious of me for some reason, and I was anxious not to attract his attentions any more than I could help. Luckily for my peace of mind, Prince Vaspian had an unholy horror of the fat little wizard and a marked aversion to his presence, and whenever they were thrown into close proximity, as during a council meeting or one of these royal feasts, he avoided the presence of Ool in a very obvious manner. Ool did not seem to take any affront at this, but merely smiled his placid, Buddha-like smile.

Hence, although we did speak and she took no notice of me whatever, I saw quite a bit of my princess during the course of these long state dinners.

Her demeanor at these feasts was proud and reserved. Although splendidly robed and adorned with flashing gems and plates of precious metals, she seemed more of a helpless prisoner than a reigning queen-to-be. She spoke little to the other women at her table. They were mostly women of the Chac Yuul, the wives or daughters or mistresses of the Black Legion chieftains, bold-eyed, barbaric, and quarrelsome. Constantly they made slighting remarks about her apparel or deportment, and went off into gales of nasty laughter at almost everything she did, until my hands ached where they gripped tightly the hilts of my sword and dagger, and I yearned to spring down among them and scatter them left and right. But I said nothing, holding my peace, sometimes with very great effort, and I do not think that any at the feast observed anything out of the way in my manner.

When she would enter or leave the hall, always on the arm of the smirking Prince, they talked in low voices. She did not hesitate to accept his arm; neither did she greet him with any perceptible animation or enthusiasm. For the life of me, I could not figure out her true feelings for Prince Vaspian. Surely, they did not act like lovers, for all that the Prince lingered over her hand, kissing it and whispering to her in a semblance of intimacy. Her features remained pale, her expression reserved, and if she did not decline speech with him, neither did she seem to welcome it with any marked pleasure.

I began to wonder if the Prince did not perhaps have some hold over her. Had he seized some advantage over her so that she did not dare openly affront him or rebuff his fawning attentions before the chieftains of the Black Legion?

For it did not seem possible that she could love him. I have no doubt but what the proud and fiery Princess of Shondakor was capable of a strong and passionate devotion, but she was too much the woman, and he too little the man, for him to have earned her love without some manner of coercion.

You can see the dilemma that confronted me.

I had gained my entrance into the city in disguise for the sole purpose of effecting her rescue. But now— how could I be certain that Darloona, in truth, *wanted* to be rescued?

And I could not help remembering how, many weeks ago, when Koja and Darloona and I were all prisoners of the wily and unscrupulous but handsome and charming Prince Thuton of Zanadar, she had willingly accepted the smoothly spoken Prince as her friend and ally and, almost, her betrothed. When Lukor and I had forcibly rescued her from his clutches, at first she was violently angry with me and denounced my assistance as unwanted. Was this adventure to be a repetition of that earlier fiasco? I could not be sure, but one thing was certain: before I attempted to free her from the hands of the Black Legion, I must hear from her own lips whether or not she was in love with Prince Vaspian.

And always before my mind's eye I saw again that terrible scene in her boudoir when she had stood, clasped in the cloaked arms of one I was convinced was none other than Vaspian, pleading passionately with him, her tear-wet cheeks and shining emerald eyes lifted to scan his visage, concealed from me by the angle at which he stood.

Had it been a love scene I had spied upon unwittingly?

If so, how could I reconcile the subdued and reserved manner of her public meetings with him, against the tempestuous emotions she had displayed when clasped in his arms in privacy?

There was simply no other course for me to follow.

I *must* have words with Darloona—and soon!

As my luck would have it, that very night an opportunity to speak privately with Darloona occurred.

Vaspian's one vice, insofar as I had yet discovered, was a fondness for a certain substance called Dream Lotus.

This was a powerful narcotic which dulled the senses and set the mind whirling free amidst a thousand gorgeous but substanceless dreams. In moments of despondency or boredom, my patron would lock himself within his private quarters, imbibe heavily of the noxious fumes of the Dream Lotus, and spend the remainder of the night sunk deep in a drugged slumber.

This night, seething with fury over some fancied slight, or perhaps due to a neurotic conviction that his faceless, and as yet unknown, foes had gained a slim ascendancy, he slunk, snarling and cursing, into his den, loudly calling for his pipe and canister of the Lotus. I was satisfied that he would not stir the remainder of the night, and thus could make no unexpected call upon my presence. Since my quarters were the outermost of all his suite, I could pretty much come or go as I pleased, and so, wrapping myself in a dark cloak, tossing my baldric over my shoulders, I set off for my long-delayed interview with Darloona.

I selected a poorly lit and seldom used corridor that wound into a virtually abandoned portion of the palace. There, in a dusty, neglected chamber, I scanned the wall for the secret sign which I had discovered to mark the sliding panels which gave one entry into the network of hidden passages wherewith these walls were tunneled.

I stifled an exclamation as the dim light of my flickering lanthorn showed the small cryptic symbol. In a moment my fingers had probed for and found the secret spring. There was a click, a grating of hidden gimbals, and a black opening yawned before me, into which I plunged without a moment's hesitation, letting the heavy arras fall behind me.

I strode with rapid yet silent steps through the winding passages within the walls of the palace. On many previous tours I had familiarized myself with the small painted signs that gave indication of direction. Thus oriented, I made my way by the shortest route to the area of the palace wherein the apartments of the Princess were situated.

My heart was in my mouth as I strode through the darkness, and I must confess my mouth was dry, my brow damp with moisture, and my heart pounding to the hurried rhythm of my throbbing pulse. It was not inconceivable that the words I would soon hear from the lips of the Princess would forever change the future of my life. For—what if she truly loved Prince Vaspian of the Black Legion? What if her impending nuptials were indeed of her own free choosing, and were not somehow being forced upon her by threats of some dire punishment?

My heart turned to lead within my breast. If such were to prove the case, then the words I should hear from the lips of the incomparable Princess I loved would be tantamount to a death sentence.

For although never yet had I spoken of my love to Darloona, and although the gap between my own lowly station and her exalted rank would likely prove an insurmountable obstacle, still in the secret places of my heart there burned, clear and pure and brilliant, the small flame of hope.

That love which is completely without hope is not love at all, but a black and bitter canker eating at the heart. Would this prove to be my doom? Did she—could she—love the Prince of the Black Legion?

The answer to this enormous question I would perhaps learn in the next few moments.

And so, with what inward trepidation I give my reader freedom to imagine for himself, I approached the passages that led to the secret spyhole and sliding panel in the wall of Darloona's apartments.

All was impenetrable gloom, yet here I must douse my lamp, for the slightest bit of light might well be visible through some crack or cranny of the walls, and it would never do to give advance warning of my presence. I could not know for certain that the Princess was alone.

Hooding my lantern under a dark cloth which I had carried for that very purpose, I went forward into utter blackness on wary, silent feet.

And froze with astonishment!

For ahead of me, limned with dim radiance against the gloom, I glimpsed the face of an unknown man.

His features were masked behind a black vizor and all that was visible was the glitter of his eyes, which were set against the spyhole in the wall. Lights from the apartment beyond dimly illuminated his profile.

Another had come to spy upon Darloona in the dark!

I drew back in mingled consternation and alarm, and I fear I stumbled slightly in the blackness, for my foot dislodged some bit of loose stone. The clatter of the stone seemed horribly loud in the utter stillness of the black passageway, and at the sound the unseen watcher snatched his face away from the peephole and, thus, vanished completely.

With drumming pulses, my breath coming in quick short gasps, I stood silent, searching the blackness with every sense for the slightest sign of my opponent's position. I could not see or hear him, but I sensed his presence. My flesh prickled and my nape hairs stirred, as if with some sixth sense I registered the pressure of invisible eyes.

Then a beam of blinding light struck me full in the eyes—a naked steel blade flashed for my heart—and in the next instant I found myself fighting for my life.

BOOK THREE

THE BOOK OF VALKAR

CHAPTER NINE

A FIGHT IN THE DARK

This was far from being the first time I had ever fought for my life, and it was not likely to be the last. But I sincerely pray to whatever gods may be that never again shall I find myself in so hopeless and desperate a situation.

A battle in the narrow confines of a secret passage is bound to be a difficult one, but when both you and your opponent are totally invisible to each other, the result is chaos.

I could hear the sound of his heavy breathing, the rasp of his buskins against the stone floor, the cling and click and slither of our swords—but in the complete darkness, I could see nothing, nothing at all!

My own sword was clear of its scabbard in a trice and I managed to engage and parry his blade to one side, but it was so close that his point drew a thread of scarlet agony across my chest, slicing through my leathern tunic. A fraction of an inch deeper and I would not be here to tell the tale.

I fought a purely defensive bout, and it took all of my science to keep that unseen sword tip from my throat. I paced backwards, step by step, yielding to his advance, and all the while I searched my wits for some way to disengage and flee—for at any instant the sound of our combat might arouse the occupants of the suites beyond the wall, and the passage might be filled with guards. My imposture would be revealed, I would be taken prisoner, and all of my hopes of giving succor to the Princess in her peril and her captivity would be dashed into the blackest depths of despair.

But, in the meantime, it was all I could do to defend myself against the attack of my invisible opponent.

Never have I fought so brilliantly as in that hour. If it had not been for the thousand tricks and tactics of advanced swordsmanship I had learned during my tutelage under the guidance of Lukor, one of the greatest swordsmen of all Thanator, I would have been slashed to ribbons or spitted upon my opponent's blade in a trice.

Whoever he was, he was a master swordsman in his own right. And this was, when I later had the leisure to ponder it, a bit puzzling. For doubtless he was some lord or warrior of the Chac Yuul, and the Chac Yuul are by no means schooled in the finer points of the art of fence. They are mounted warriors, for the most part, used to chopping away with heavy cutlass-like cavalry weapons, and far more familiar with the uses of spear, battle-ax, and morning star, than with the rapier. Yet my opponent was a marvelous swordsman of consummate skill and of a degree of science that came near to equaling my own. And, with all due modesty, I may safely claim to be one of the finest swordsmen on all of this jungle world of terror and mystery.

The duel was fast and furious, but it did not occupy very much time. In fact, it was over in a few seconds.

For I had backed by now into the corridor, and yielding before the furious assault of my unseen foe, suddenly I stumbled again—this time over my own lantern—and fell flat on my back.

In falling, my foot tore away the cloth whereby I had shielded the glow of my lantern. The sudden burst of brilliant light must have bedazzled and even temporarily blinded my foeman, for his blade faltered, and although he could probably have put a length of steel through my breast as I sprawled prone and momentarily stunned, he blundered.

In the next instant I sprang to one knee and my own blade flashed in a lucky stroke. So dazzled was he by the sudden flare of illumination that he did not parry the stroke and the tip of my steel caught him in a shallow cut across the cheek, just below the black silken vizor that masked his unknown features.

It was only a slight scratch, but it would nevertheless take some days to heal, and it occurred to me that should I chance to encounter my unknown assailant in the next few days, I should be able to identify him by the wound.

Seizing the opportunity for flight, he sprang backwards, ducked into a side branch of the secret passage, and was gone in an instant.

I sprang to my feet, ready to give pursuit, but the sound of clattering footsteps came to my ears and I heard curt, questioning voices and the clank and clamor of metal accouterments, and knew that someone had heard the sounds of our duel in the dark and had given the alarm, summoning the guards.

Thus it was that I hastily retraced my steps to avoid the chance of discovery. And I did not that night, after all, have the opportunity to hear from the lips of my beloved princess whether or not she had truly given her heart into the keeping of another.

For the next day or two Prince Vaspian kept me busy to such an extent that it was impossible for me to contrive a private interview with the Princess.

The morning following my duel in the dark against a mysterious foe I scrutinized the Prince's features closely, without appearing to do so, and was curiously relieved to discover his face innocent of the slightest scratch. I say "relieved," but actually my emotions were somewhat more mixed. I knew the Prince knew little of the art of fence, and thus it did not seem likely that it was the son of Arkola with whom I had battled in the black gloom of the secret passage, for whoever my unknown opponent had been, he was a brilliant swordsman of superb skills.

And yet, since it had been the Prince who had instructed me in my first knowledge of the secret passages, I knew that he was well aware of them; and as Darloona had once been mistress of all this palace, and presumably was privy to a knowledge of the network of passages within her own walls, and since I believed the two of them were lovers, he was the most likely candidate to have been my nameless foe. For I had yet to encounter another person in my explorations of the secret passages.

Two days after my duel in the dark Prince Vaspian required me to attend him at a court function of such importance that his presence was commanded by the Usurper. Certain officers of the Black Legion were to receive acclamation for their bravery or ability at command, and all the lords of the Chac Yuul were required to be present.

The function took place in a mighty hall, high-ceilinged and lit by a thousand tapers. The hall was thronged with barbaric warriors and splendid chieftains adorned in all their wealth of savage finery, and among them all the Prince my patron shone in the jeweled splendor of his raiment. Nodding plumes crowned his burnished helm, gems glittered from the hilt of his sword, and badges and honors of precious metals encrusted his tunic and girdle.

As he circled the hall, I paced silently behind him, a pace or two to the rear. My stay in the Black Legion had not yet covered a sufficient interval of time for me to have made the acquaintance of any of these chieftains, and thus it was with some surprise that I felt a hand clap me on the shoulder and turned about to meet a friendly smile in a familiar face.

"Ah, Jandar, it is a pleasure to greet you again!" cried a warm voice, and I realized that it was my former comrade and commander, Valkar of Ganatol.

"How do you like palace duty?" he inquired. "Some-

what different, I am certain, from the hard life of barracks and practice field, eh?" He laughed and I forced
a smile, but ere we could exchange more than a few
words my Prince shrilly demanded my presence, dart-
ing a suspicious glance at Valkar, and I was forced to
bid the *komor* a hasty adieu.

"Some night when you can get free, meet me at the
wineshop beside the forum—do you recall the place
where we shared a bottle after the theater that night?"
he called. I smiled and nodded, but had to turn away
for the Prince's hand was on my arm and his jealous
eyes were taking in every detail of my chance acquaintance.

"Who is that fellow to whom you spoke?" he hissed.

"It is the chieftain Valkar under whom I served in
the third cohort, Lord—surely you recall questioning
him about my record of service, after I was lucky
enough to halt your runaway thaptors?"

"Ah, yes; I remember him now," he muttered, and
the light of jealousy and suspicion died from his
pinched, sharp features; however he retained his
clutch on my arm. "Do not stray away from my side
again, Jandar; I require your constant attendance, for
here I am virtually surrounded by those who call themselves my friends but who secretly plot behind my
back."

I nodded and obediently fell into place behind him,
and it was all that I could do to keep a wooden expression on my features. Shock, astonishment, and surprise whirled through my brain.

For it would have been indeed a pleasure to renew
my friendship with the gallant, gentlemanly Valkar,
had it not been for the scratch on his cheek—*the
scratch my sword had made two nights before, when
we had battled in the dark!*

The remainder of that festive evening is but a blur
to me. Strive as I may, I can recall but a giddy pano-
rama of plumed warriors and beautiful women. Re-

sounding speeches were made and toasts were drunk, but I recall neither the speeches nor those whom the toasts saluted.

For I could not expunge from my mind that it was Valkar whom I had battled in the darkness of the secret passage—Valkar whom I had surprised in the very act of spying upon the apartment of the Princess Darloona—Valkar who had been prowling the secret passages, masked and cloaked, in the darkness of the night!

After returning to my quarters following the close of the festivities, I disrobed and stretched out on my bed, but sleep came not easily to me. My mind was a bewildered turmoil of unanswered questions and unsolved mysteries.

I remember that night at the theater to which Valkar had made reference, and I recalled the strange intensity of his gaze and the pallor of his features as he gazed upon Darloona, seated at the side of Prince Vaspian in the royal box.

At the time his tension and the alertness of his gaze had puzzled me, but only slightly, and in the flow of events I had all but forgotten the incident, which seemed in retrospect of little importance. But now I was no longer certain just how important it might have been.

And I recalled, as well, an incident in that wineshop to which Valkar had also referred, the wineshop to which we had repaired after the play. The chance stumbling of a servant wench had spilled wine upon the features of my companion, and in wiping his face he had accidentally wiped away some of the swarthy hue of his features. And thus it seemed that Valkar, even as I, was an impostor.

Tossing and turning on my bed, unable to slumber, I puzzled over these baffling mysteries and wondered exactly who and what my friend Valkar really was, and what was his true reason for joining the Black Legion?

And even more important—was he my friend, or my foe?

Long had I anticipated a private interview with Darloona and the opportunity came about at last, but in the most unexpected manner possible.

The impending nuptials of Vaspian and Darloona were now very close. Only a week remained before they would solemnize their vows before the idol of the dark god worshiped by the Chac Yuul barbarians.

And yet another deadline was drawing close, as well. For the ultimatum delivered by Prince Thuton to the Black Legion was almost due for its answer. Thuton demanded a mighty ransom for surrendering his interests in the person of the Princess of Shondakor, and in default of the prompt payment of that price he had sworn to bring the awesome aerial navy of Zanadar down upon the city in war. Soon, very soon, the lords of the Black Legion must decide upon a course of action.

And so must I. For I could not plan any rescue of Darloona until I had heard from her own lips whether she was being forced into marriage with Prince Vaspian, or whether she truly had given him her heart and hand. But how could I get to see her?

The solution to my dilemma came from, of all persons, Prince Vaspian, himself!

He hailed me, a day or so after my chance encounter with Valkar, and bade me attend him.

"Soon, as you know, the Princess Darloona and I shall be wed," he said, and I inwardly writhed in revulsion at the oily, self-satisfied smirk wherewith he accompanied his words. "I have a small gift for my bride-to-be; generally, my tokens are delivered by the hand of my confidential valet, Golar, as you must know; alas, he is busy on another errand this evening, so I entrust the task to you."

I suppressed, with some difficulty, the exclamation of delight which rose to my lips. I do not think that so

much as a flicker of surprise or eagerness crossed my
features, although within my heart I was shaken by
this sudden flash of good fortune. And I am positive
that Prince Vaspian observed nothing of my feelings.

"As my prince commands," I said quietly.

He smirked. "There's a good fellow!" Then he
pressed into my hands a gorgeous ornament that
blazed with precious gems unknown to me and gave
me minute directions so that I might find my way to
the secluded chambers wherein the Princess dwelt, and
a note from his hand that would get me past the
guards.

I should explain that while Darloona was not tech-
nically a prisoner, she was kept under the closest possible watch and no one might gain entrance into her
presence without passing the examination of those
watchers assigned to guard her. This surveillance
aside, she was permitted the greatest latitude and
could command whatever she wished.

Without delay I made my way to her suite by the
shortest possible route. As I approached her quarters
my heart was thumping like that of a foolish school-
boy on his first date, my mouth was dry, and I was
mentally composing my speech to her.

The guards stationed at her door halted me, ex-
amined the Prince's sign manual which I carried, and
became extremely uncomfortable.

"*Komad,* we mean no affront to our lord the Prince,
but the Lady Darloona has given us express instruction
that she be not disturbed this evening. Since the Warlord, Arkola, has commanded us to obey the Princess
in all things, save permitting her to elude surveillance,
we thus cannot allow you to pass."

"But it is a message from her betrothed!" I protested.
"And surely the Princess cannot have retired to her
couch so early in the evening as this. Can you not—"

The officer shook his head with reluctant firmness.

"We are not permitted to transgress against her

wishes in such matters," he said. "It is the command of the Lord Arkola that she be given the illusion of freedom and that her privacy be not intruded upon, save in matters of the most dire necessity. We must, therefore, refuse to let you pass."

My face reddened. "But I am expressly commanded by Prince Vaspian to deliver this gift—"

"And I am expressly commanded by the Lord of the Black Legion to obey the wishes of the Princess," he said curtly. Then, misunderstanding my distress as a rather natural fear of returning to my patron with his commands unfulfilled, he softened: "You can, of course, leave the gift with me and I shall see that it is delivered into the hands of the Princess personally. Or you may simply return tomorrow morning and deliver it yourself."

I was seized by a fury of impatience and frustration, but I could not afford to argue. For how could I explain that if I waited till tomorrow, the Prince's confidential valet, Golar, would be back on duty and since a task of this nature was usually assigned to him, I would thus lose my one opportunity to seek a private interview with Darloona without risk of arousing the suspicions of the Chac Yuul?

As there was no recourse, I nodded and turned away, but the turmoil in my breast was such that I did not go far. It was perfectly infuriating to be this close to my goal and unable to progress a single step further.

On sudden impulse I turned aside into certain seldom-used side passages and followed them, searching for the unobtrusive sign which I knew denoted a sliding panel which would give me entrance into the system of secret passages within the palace walls.

Ere I had gone far I found that for which I sought. A swift glance revealed I was alone and unobserved. My fingers found and depressed a spring concealed in the carven detail of the wall. A panel slid ajar and I stepped into the darkness.

Without difficulty, so familiar had I become with the system of secret passages by this time, I made my way to the apartments of the Princess. My hand was upon the spring that would open a panel and give me entrance into her boudoir, but a sudden flash of caution bade me survey the room before entering it so abruptly. I found the nearest spyhole, slid aside its cover, and set my eye thereto, peering into the room.

To my astonishment, once more I found myself gazing upon my beloved in the arms of another. A tall man, cloaked and hooded in dark green—surely, it was the same man whom once before I had discovered thus engaged in a tender embrace with the Princess Darloona—a man whom I felt certain was none other than my patron, Prince Vaspian, himself.

But this was most peculiar indeed! Why on earth—or on Thanator, for that matter—would Vaspian have gone out of his way to send me to the Princess with his gift when he was en route to her quarters himself and could easily have delivered the jewelry in person? It simply did not make sense!

Alas, while I stood paralyzed with astonishment at this most puzzling and unexpected development, the hooded man turned swiftly from the embrace of Darloona, bade her farewell, thumbed the spring, and opened the sliding panel.

Before I could rouse myself to action—before I could move away into the dark recesses of the passage or even think of so doing, the secret door opened, bathing me in the light of the room and the cloaked and hooded figure stepped into the passage where I stood frozen and confronted me face to face.

For a moment we both stood motionless, gripped by the surprise of this sudden and unexpected encounter.

Then Darloona's lover forced an unsteady laugh, and said, "Doubtless, friend, you are thinking the same thing, but—whatever are *you* doing here, Jandar?"

CHAPTER TEN

VALKAR UNMASKED!

It was not Prince Vaspian at all, but *Valkar!* By the light of the small lantern he carried I could see him quite clearly, the guarded expression of his face, and the way his right hand hovered rather near the hilt of his rapier.

It should not have come as such a surprise as it did. I should really have been prepared for this discovery. After all, had I not encountered Valkar, masked, peering into the Princess' suite some days earlier? Had I not marked his face with my sword during that terrible duel in the dark, and had I not identified him as my unknown assailant at the court function, when I saw the fresh scar on his unmasked face?

However, I had by now convinced myself that the cloaked man I had seen holding Darloona in his arms was my patron, Prince Vaspian; and such is the power of self-conviction that it had not even entered my mind that her lover might be someone else. Now that I began to see things in their true light, I realized that the Prince and Valkar were about the same height and build, and that they wore cloaks of identical design and hue, which was not surprising, as most warriors of the Chac Yuul wore cloaks of this design—I had one, myself—and the hair of both was sleek and black.

Valkar saw the blank expression of surprise on my face, and the tension left his handsome features. He laughed and clapped me on the shoulder. "But we cannot converse here, where the guards beyond Darloona's door may hear the muffled tones of conversation and become alarmed. Indeed, it is surprising that they did not become earlier alarmed at our recent sword duel—for now I believe that it was you, Jandar, who surprised me peering into the apartments of the Princess to see if she was alone, and who gave me this small scar on the face! Come, I know a place nearby where we can be alone and where no one is likely to overhear us."

He led me to a secluded chamber which, from the accumulated dust and other tokens of neglect, was very seldom visited. There he lit a half-consumed candle in a silver holder, threw off his cloak, and turned to regard me with a half serious and half humorous gaze.

"I suspect, old friend, that you are here for much the same reason as I—to effect the escape of the Princess Darloona," he said.

"I am. It was for that reason alone that I entered Shondakor and sought a place in the fighting forces of the Chac Yuul," I admitted. He nodded.

"It is the same with me. But I do not recognize you as a defender of the cause of the rightful queen of Shondakor," he mused. "Never do I recall having seen you at the court of the Princess, nor even as being among the warrior nobles who fled into the Grand Kumala with the Princess when the treacherous arts of Ool the Uncanny permitted the Black Legion to enter and seize the city. Why, then, this desperate mission? Who *are* you, Jandar?"

"I am not a Shondakorian, but a stranger from a far-off land," I admitted. "I am the man who assisted the Princess to escape from the clutches of the Yathoon Horde when they took her prisoner in the jungle country; and, still later, when she was held captive by Prince Thuton of Zanadar, it was I, together with a friendly renegade Yathoon chieftain named Koja and a gallant old Swordmaster from Ganatol named Lukor, who rescued her from the Cloud City of the Sky Pirates, only to lose her to a patrol of Black Legion war-

riors. Since her present captivity by the Chac Yuul is
in part my own fault, I resolved to gain a place in the
Legion and see if I could not undo my failure to adequately protect her by yet once again effecting her
freedom and returning her to her people. Thus I disguised my identity with a false history even as you,
Valkar, are disguised with cosmetics! For I know that
you are truly a Shondakorian, a man of the Ku Thad,
and that the color of your skin and hair is false."

This fact that I knew he was disguised came as a
bit of a shock to Valkar, and I think that it was this,
that I had known for some time of his disguise and
had not ever revealed it to the authorities, that convinced him that I was a friend and a defender of the
Princess. He blinked, his expression sobering.

"How long have you known this?" he asked slowly.

"Ever since that night in the wineshop when the
serving wench spilled wine on you, erasing some of
your false skin-coloring," I said. He nodded grimly.

"Against such accidents no man can adequately
guard," he admitted. "I recall the incident well; since
you made no remark, and gave no sign of having noticed, I assumed that I had managed to repair the
damage to my makeup before you observed."

Then his eyes grew thoughtful and he laughed.

"Is it not odd how fate plays small tricks upon we
mortals? You and I, I think, instinctively liked and
trusted each other and soon became fast friends—both
of us spies, infiltrating the ranks of the Black Legion
for the same purpose, but neither aware that the other
was here for the same reason as himself! It is almost as
if our secret sympathy and common cause communicated by some sixth sense, finding a kindred soul to
which it felt drawn for unknown reasons." Then he
shrugged and a friendly smile warmed his sober features.

"For all these months I have been here in Shondakor, unable to effect Darloona's rescue, although I did
manage to win a high rank among the host of the Chac

Yuul. Whereas you, Jandar, enter the Legion and almost at once attract the patronage of that sneaking
horeb,* Prince Vaspian, and are able to come and go in
the palace as you please, where I can gain entrance
only by the most extraordinary use of caution and
agility. I congratulate you on your good fortune! Between the two of us, we may be able to render aid to
our Princess."

"If she truly desires our aid," said I, gloomily. He
asked my meaning with some surprise, and I recounted
to him something of my own suspicions regarding
Darloona—suspicions that had been roused by her
ambiguous behavior with Prince Vaspian and by her
seemingly willing acceptance of his suit. I pointed out
reluctantly that I could see no reason why a woman
so fiercely proud as Darloona should accept the cowardly and psychotic Vaspian as her consort-to-be unless, by some incredible chance, she had actually fallen
in love with the son of Arkola.

"Darloona," I concluded glumly, "is no tender
maiden to be frightened into a marriage by threats of
punishment. She is strong-willed, a warrior princess if
ever there was one, and I cannot believe that she
would permit any threatened danger to force her into
a marriage where love was not. Indeed, I can hardly
imagine any threat that could coerce the Princess of
the Ku Thad into a wedding with that whining little
monster. Unlikely as it seems, she must truly love
him!"

He listened to my suspicions with a meditative
mien. My reasoning was now somewhat shaken, you
will perceive, by the discovery that it was not Vaspian
I had surprised in a clandestine embrace with the

---

* In another place, Captain Dark explains that a *horeb* is a
repulsive scavenger of disgusting appearance and even more
disgusting habits. It is, in fact, the Thanatorian equivalent of
a "rat," and like the terrene rodent it so closely resembles, its
name has become a derogatory synonym for a skulking, treacherous person.—L.C.

Princess of Shondakor in the seclusion of her boudoir, but Valkar himself: yet it was true that she had accepted him as her betrothed and that she did not publicly repulse the affections of the Prince. So her behavior in this regard was still a mystery to me.

When I had finished, Valkar wasted no time in setting me to rights on this point.

"Let me relieve your mind on this question, Jandar, my friend," he said vigorously. "The Princess loathes and despises Prince Vaspian as any proud and noble woman of her high birth and breeding could. She has told me that she would rather sheathe a dagger in her heart than accept the hand of Vaspian before the dark altars of the Chac Yuul."

I looked at him with some surprise.

"If this be so," I mused, "why then does she not repudiate her promise to wed the Prince?"

His voice was somber and his eyes smoldered with repressed fires as he explained the puzzle.

"She *dares* not. For Vaspian holds the key to the safety of her people. You see, the policies of the Black Legion are decided by a consensus of the high council of the Lords of the Legion, one of whom is Prince Vaspian."

"So I have been given to understand." I nodded.

"And, hitherto, whenever the question arose of whether it would not be wise for the Legion to protect its rather shaky and insecure control over the citizens of Shondakor by mass executions and imprisonment—a logical, if cold-blooded, course of action which Arkola himself approves most heartily—Prince Vaspian holds the deciding vote, for the council is neatly divided upon this question."

"But why should Vaspian object? Surely, not from any humanitarian considerations, for he is as cold-blooded as the rest of them."

"True." Valkar smiled grimly. "But Vaspian hates his father and wherever possible opposes him in public measures out of sheer spitefulness. Hence he has al-

ways cast his vote against the measure in the past,
whenever it has come up on the agenda of the council
meetings. But he has threatened Darloona in secret
that if she does not agree to become his bride, he will
raise the matter again and this time cast his vote upon
his father's side. It is virtually the only way the Prince
can injure his father, whom he hates for being more of
a man than himself, and he takes great delight from
openly frustrating Arkola's will. And against this sort
of rebellion, of course, even so powerful a leader as
the Warlord is helpless, due to the very laws of the
Black Legion, and their customs and traditions."*

I nodded, remembering the open hostility I had observed between Vaspian and Arkola at the council
meeting I had attended some days ago.

Valkar continued: "As for Darloona, the only thing
the unhappy girl can do to prevent the mass slaughter
of her helpless people is to promise to wed the slimy
little monster. Thus she dares not repulse his attentions in public."

Why had I never thought of this logical answer to
the mystery of her behavior? As the true realization of
Darloona's ghastly plight burst upon me, cold sweat
bedewed my brow and I tasted the metallic, bitterness
of dread.

* If my reader finds it difficult to understand why so strongly
willed and supremely powerful a man as Arkola could be completely helpless in this situation, let me call your attention to
what Captain Dark said earlier about the unique traditions of
the Chac Yuul. Arkola is an elected leader, chosen from among
the various clans and tribes of the free Black Legion warriors
to lead them, and his will is unquestioned and his commands
obeyed, but only so long as a majority vote of the high council
of the Legion supports him. Were a majority of the council members to oppose him, he could be voted from his high office
and another chosen in his place. Neither hereditary monarch
born to power nor a general commanding by virtue of seniority,
Arkola rules only so long as the clan chiefs desire him to do so.
This is why Vaspian is able to openly defy his father's wishes,
and why Arkola is helpless to discipline the Prince.—L.C.

Of course it was impossible that Darloona could have given her love to the cowardly, whining Prince!

But it was equally impossible that, even with the aid of my newfound ally, Valkar, I could ever persuade Darloona to escape the city with me. For the vengeful and malicious Vaspian would punish her betrayal of him by bringing about the mass execution of the unarmed and captive populace—and she knew it!

Was there ever a dilemma so completely hopeless?

There was utterly nothing that I could do to prevent the woman I loved from marrying the man she loathed and despised from the very bottom of her proud heart.

After a time I roused myself from these grim thoughts and queried my friend Valkar, asking if he had any ideas as to how we could help Darloona resolve her problems.

He shrugged gloomily.

"None whatsoever," he admitted. "Ever since I managed to locate the secret entrance into the palace, whereby to effect my secret interviews with the Princess, I have begged her to flee the city by my side, but to no avail. It is impossible for her to consider such an action, for to do so would mean that she dooms to death the very people who love and trust her, and whom she has sworn to protect. Alas, my poor cousin! She is helpless in such a situation."

"Cousin?" I asked.

"Why, yes. I thought you knew—how stupid of me not to explain who I am. My name really is Valkar, but as you know I am not a Ganatolian, but a prince of the Ku Thad. My father is Lord Yarrak, the Uncle of the Princess, and the leader of the Ku Thad during her captivity."

"I see; yes, I know Lord Yarrak well, he has been my host for some weeks, prior to my joining the Black Legion. Odd that he never mentioned a son—especially

a son who had infiltrated the Black Legion in disguise
—when he knew I was planning the same sort of thing
myself!"

"Not at all, Jandar. My father doubtless believes
that I am dead, long since slain in the street fighting
when the Chac Yuul first entered the city months ago.
We became separated in the confusion, and when the
warrior nobles escaped from the city, bearing the
Princess away to the safety of the jungles, I remained
behind. I was protected by friends among the common folk and stayed in hiding for some time, until
matters quieted down. Before I managed to make my
escape, the Princess had been captured, and so I remained here without seeking to join my father and my
people. Friends in the city helped me disguise my
golden skin and flame-red hair, and as a Ganatolian
mercenary I gained a place in the ranks of the conquerors, hoping to assist the Princess, my betrothed, to
escape later on—"

I fear some involuntary exclamation must have escaped my lips as Valkar spoke these words.

He broke off, staring at me.

"Why, what is it, Jandar? What is the matter? What
have I said to disturb you? Why, man, you are white
to the lips!"

I forced my features into a semblance of calm and
steadied my voice with a considerable effort of will.

"Your—*betrothed?*" I repeated in a low voice.

He shrugged a little and laughed in a self-
deprecating way.

"Why—yes. The Princess and I have been betrothed since our childhood. A formal alliance of the
two major branches of the blood royal—you understand; that sort of thing."

"I did not know," I said faintly. I felt exactly like a
man who had just been kicked in the stomach. And I
hope it did not show.

"In Shondakorian custom," he went on idly, "a
prince or a princess of the royal house will very often

be pledged to marry his or her cousin from earliest ages. Darloona and I would most likely have been married by now had not the Chac Yuul invasion somewhat disrupted the normal flow of events." He chuckled ruefully at this enormous understatement.

"But whatever is it, Jandar? Didn't you know that Darloona and I were to wed?"

"In all truth, no."

He laughed helplessly. "But, surely you must realize that only the fact that Darloona is to be my queen would force me to this dangerous extremity! Only to save my bride-to-be would I take such enormous risks as trying to maintain this masquerade and walk in disguise among the very ranks of they who are my enemies and the enemies of my house."

I nodded wordlessly. I knew exactly what he meant.

And thus was I struck down into the very depths of despair, as must any man be, when he discovers that his best friend also loves the woman whom *he* loves, and has, in fact, already won her love and her promise of marriage!

All these long months of being hopelessly in love with a woman who despised me, who considered me a coward, a fumbler, and a fool—I thought I knew by now what hell was like.

But I had yet to learn what hell could *really* be!

CHAPTER ELEVEN

IN THE DEPTHS OF DESPAIR

Yes, I knew what Valkar meant when he said that only his great love for the Princess would have driven him to take such a desperate risk as venturing into the very ranks of the Black Legion in disguise.

I knew it all too well! For I, too, loved Darloona with a hopeless and consuming passion. My devotion to her was almost beyond the ability of words to describe. And only the fact that the woman I loved, the peerless Princess to whom I had given my heart, was in terrible danger would have driven me to the desperate extremity of penetrating the conquered city as an impostor.

Of course I knew exactly what Valkar meant! For I had been driven by the same emotion to risk precisely the same dangers as had he.

I thank God that the parallel did not occur to him, but of course he could have no reason to suspect that my devotion to Darloona was spurred by a passion identical to his own. Had he known this, I think I would have died of shame.

Neither he nor Darloona must ever have reason to suspect that I love her. Never by word or deed, by look or glance, must I permit either my best friend or the woman I love to guess the depths of my adoration.

It is a foolish passion, I admitted, that I, a homeless and wandering adventurer, a stranger come by chance or accident from another world, a lowly born member

of an alien race, dared to love the splendid Princess of
Shondakor—what a mockery!

I had known that my love was a hopeless one, of
course; known it even before discovering that Darloona had sworn to wed Prince Vaspian of the Black
Legion. Her contempt for me, freely expressed upon
many occasions; her unfortunate experiences at my
bungling and incompetent hands; these and many
other factors had given an indication to me that I had
been most foolish to admit my love, even to myself!

And so my position had long been a hopeless one.
But worse was yet to come!

For the hopelessness of my situation was only in-
creased by a feeling of horror and dread, when I came
to realize that the woman I loved was being forced
into a marriage with a man she despised—a marriage
which she dared not oppose or avoid.

But now I had truly descended into the depths of
despair.

For if Valkar and Darloona were in love, and sworn
to each other, how could I hope to win the woman of
my dreams, even if by some miracle I managed to free
her from her vows to Vaspian and from the captivity
of the Chac Yuul?

Black, bitter depression filled my aching heart. For I
remembered that glimpse through the spyhole. I had
seen Valkar with Darloona clasped in a passionate embrace, I had seen her shining eyes lifted to his, her
tear-wet cheeks, and had heard the soft warmth of her
pleading voice.

I had thought that my only friend in the city of
Shondakor was now my accomplice and ally in the
task of freeing the woman I loved from those that
held her prisoner. And now it seemed that he was my
rival for her heart. Nay, no rival, but already the victor in the unequal contest, for he had long since won
her love.

And I wished that I had never set foot on the jun-

gled surface of this strange and terrible and beautiful
world, and that I had never looked upon Darloona,
Warrior Princess of the Ku Thad!

The next day or two passed by without any occur-
rence of note. I fear I went about my duties like a
mindless automaton, or a somnambulist. I hardly managed to pay attention to the things which went on
around me. So deeply was I plunged into a black
mood of utter despair that my drugged condition and
leaden mood must have been obvious to everyone
who encountered me. I responded with dull monosyl-
labic replies whenever anyone chanced to speak to me.
I must have looked like a man stricken by some horrible discovery, some overwhelming calamity.

And that is precisely what I was.

But fortunately the Prince my patron dwelt secluded from the more populous sectors of the palace,
and as my duties were few and I remained in my
room most of the time, few if any could have noticed
my depression.

Concluding my secret meeting with Prince Valkar
of Shondakor, and without seeking an interview with
the Princess Darloona, since it was now futile even to
hope, I returned to Vaspian's suite.

The Prince was greatly annoyed that I had not been
able to obey his wishes and deliver the trinket to his
betrothed, but it was a matter of the smallest importance, and the following morning, when Golar had returned to his duties, he dispatched his confidential
valet with the ornament and that was that.

Usually alert and sensitive to the slightest moods of
those around him, because of his psychotic fears of
plots and spies and his consuming suspicions of the
motives of everyone he encountered, the Prince was
so caught up in the last-minute preparations for his
impending nuptials, now mere days in the future, that
I strongly doubt if even he noticed anything out of the
way in my behavior. At any rate I saw little of him

and spent most of the time in my room, busy with my
doleful thoughts.

I believe there can hardly be a more terrible situation in the human condition than to discover that your
closest friend has wooed and won the heart of the
woman you secretly love. I, at least, have never before
tasted such black bitterness, and I pray to the unknown Lords of Gordrimator, whom the Thanatorians
call gods, that I never taste such again.

Valkar and I parted on pledges of mutual assistance,
and we arranged to meet secretly a few days before
the wedding of Darloona and Prince Vaspian.

What this meeting was supposed to accomplish, I do
not believe either of us knew. But as a last-minute attempt to rescue the woman we both loved from the
grim results of her folly, we hoped to arrive at some
solution to the dark dilemma in which we were im-
mersed.

It may well be that Prince Valkar had thought of
the same possible solution to our mutual problem
which had also occurred to me. For there was *one*
way out of this corner.

Prince Vaspian could—die.

Never have I slain a man in cold blood, and I did
not face the prospect with any particular joy. Although the Prince disgusted me, and the manner in
which he smirked and strutted and preened himself
over his so-called "conquest" of the most beautiful
woman of all Thanator stung me to a fury of loathing, he was personally weak and vain, frivolous and
ineffectual—and I could not consider the slaying of
such a weakling as anything more noble than sheer
murder.

I have always considered myself a man of honor.
But like all men, I have once or twice in my life done
something of which I was not proud. To strike down
this smirking fool in cold blood, to pit my vastly superior skill with the sword against his feeble arm and
uncertain hand, would be rank cowardice.

Yet I must do it, if I wished to save Darloona from his unclean lust.

I wrestled with my conscience during those black, bitter hours. Just how much did I owe this woman, who did not return my love and was to wed my friend? Must I stain my honor with cold-blooded and cowardly murder for a woman who, after all, despised me?

To this torrent of doubts, there was only one answer possible.

I owed Darloona everything that I could give her, even the sacrifice of my unstained honor, or my very life, if she should require it. And I did not have the right to demand so much as the favor of a single smile in return.

For when a man loves, he loves wholly, he withholds nothing of himself, or it is not truly love. This sort of chivalry may sound old-fashioned, and perhaps it is, but my love for her was beyond any question of payment or price.

And thus I agonized for days. My situation rapidly became all but intolerable. Valkar was my closest friend, my confidant, my coconspirator. That he had won the love of my peerless Princess should not have caused me pain, for whom better should Darloona marry than a man like Valkar?

He was brave, intelligent, noble, and strong. He was a brilliant officer, a mighty prince, and his mission here in entering the city of the Chac Yuul in disguise, in a desperate one-man attempt to rescue the woman he loved from the very stronghold of her enemies, was heroic almost to the point of madness.

Why, then, should I begrudge him the love of the most beautiful woman of two worlds? Because of my own selfish passion?

It was absurd! My own love for Darloona was strong and deep and sincere, and it would endure to my last heartbeat. I would adore Darloona and fight for her while a single breath remained in my body, while a single drop of blood remained to animate my flesh.

But I was not even nobly born, much less a powerful prince, heir to a kingly house and a great fortune. My passion for her was hopeless. Darloona needed a man beside her on the throne who had been trained since childhood to rule. Such a man, of course, was Valkar. I could just imagine what kind of a prince consort *I* would make! Why, what did I know about being a king? The only thing I knew how to do was pilot a helicopter—and get myself into trouble: I had a real talent for doing that.

But I am as human as the next fellow, and I fear that I was often rather curt, sullen, and incommunicative with Valkar whenever we met to consider the various possible ways we could rescue Darloona from her impending marriage.

I did not mention the possibility of slaying Prince Vaspian. The onus for such a crime must rest on me alone; Valkar must know nothing of it in advance. When the time came, when it became necessary—I should simply do it.

Thus things went on for some days and the time of the marriage came near.

And then the most extraordinary accident occurred. To this hour I can remember the lift of my spirits, and the amazement which accompanied this resurgence. Valkar, I am sure, knew nothing of what was happening within me, although my depression and sullen spirits must have been obvious to all.

We were sitting in a corner table sharing a bottle of wine. Such was my preoccupation that I had thoughtlessly let fall some reference to Darloona's love for Valkar, and of the strength of his emotion for her.

He looked surprised for just a moment, and then

voiced a rather apologetic laugh.

"I fear that you have misconstrued my words, Jandar," he said awkwardly.

"How is that?"

"Why—all this talk of how much Darloona loves me. We are, of course, the very best of friends, and have been ever since our childhood. But, alas, we do not *love* each other."

He laughed, a trifle sadly.

"Ours is, as I thought you must surely understand, a marriage of political alliance. As far as I know, Darloona has never yet been in love with me, or anyone else."

"And you—?"

He grinned a bit wearily.

"Oh, I shall make her the finest husband possible, and I admire and like her enormously, but I have never been in love with her."

"But I saw you clasped in each other's arms—I saw her lift tear-stained cheeks and pleading eyes to your face!"

"That must have been when she was begging me to flee from the city and get out before my imposture was discovered," he said idly. "She was in an agony of apprehension lest I be found out and punished, on her account. But here, Jandar! You have turned white as death again! Are you all right, old friend?"

I suppose the shock of this wonderful discovery must have been visible on my features, but I know that Valkar could not have known the depth of joy in my heart.

The woman I loved was yet heart-free—and I could hope, at least!

CHAPTER TWELVE

AN UNEXPECTED MEETING

The next day or two Prince Vaspian kept me busy in the palace and I had no time for any further meetings with my fellow conspirator. But we had arranged a last-minute rendezvous at the wineshop, to take place just a couple of hours before the wedding, which was to be solemnized at the hour of midday.

At this last meeting we planned to coordinate our efforts to rescue Darloona, and, although I feel certain that Valkar did not suspect it, part of my own plans for that fateful hour included the cold-blooded murder of Prince Vaspian.

The day arrived.

The palace was a bustle of preparations; Vaspian preened and strutted like a peacock, leered and smirked over his impending nuptials until I grimly realized that it would be not at all unpleasant to put a yard of steel through his despicable heart.

The time for my rendezvous approached. Vaspian had no particular need of me until the hour of the ceremony arrived, and so I did not find it difficult to make my way through the palace to the nearest exit.

Whatever Valkar and I should decide to do, my own plans were fixed and certain. The task of playing the assassin was mine; it could only be mine, for only I could come and go freely in the private apartments of the Prince; only I had the opportunity to request a private audience with him immediately prior to our departure for the Hall of Hoom, as the devil god of the Chac Yuul was known, before whose high altar the nuptials would be celebrated by Ool the wizard-priest.

And at that private audience I would accomplish the murder and be gone; such was to be my lonely fate.

Or so I thought at the time!

But *va lu rokka,* as the fatalistic philosophy of the Yathoon hordesmen has it. That which is destined shall come to pass, whatever your plans may be.

And, as things turned out, it was not after all my destiny to meet with Valkar at the wineshop that morning.

Fate had a few surprises in store for Jandar of Callisto!

It was my plan to leave the royal citadel by a side entrance which, while well guarded, was rather neglected. Few used it, as most of the lords and chieftains of the Black Legion preferred the more accessible main gate. But as my mission was of a somewhat surreptitious nature, and I did not desire to attract any more attention than I could help, I chose to leave by this side gate. And it is upon just such small matters as these, the passing whims of a moment, that the fate of empires and the destiny of worlds sometimes hang.

For as I strode through the gate, nodding at the guards who knew me for Prince Vaspian's man, I encountered a Chac Yuul war party entering the palace with two prisoners in tow. When I glanced with casual curiosity at the two captives, I got the surprise of my life.

For they were my old comrades, Koja and Lukor!

Koja, the towering Yathoon, loomed above the squat Black Legion warriors by head, shoulders, and upper thorax. His bare, glistening, chitinous forelimbs were bound behind him with tough leather thongs. His bald, ovoid head, crowned with segmented feelers, bore only the slightest resemblance to a human visage. His horny, immobile face and huge solemn eyes

were physiologically incapable of registering changes
of emotion, and he regarded me with an unfathomable
gaze.

As for Lukor, the peppery little Swordmaster of
Zanadar was somewhat the worse for wear. His
somber-colored garments were torn, dirtied, and disheveled. His shock of snowy hair was disarranged. He
was bleeding from a number of small scratches and
minor cuts, and I have no doubt that those who had
captured him had not done so without discovering
that it is not an easy thing to disarm a swordsman of
such masterly skill. His face was stiff and expressionless as he saw me, but from the flash of excitement in
his eyes I knew that he had instantly recognized me
despite the unexpectedness of our meeting.

As for myself, I fear I retained less composure than
did my two old friends. I believe I paled, and an expression of shocked surprise doubtless crossed my features at this unexpected meeting.

The *komad* in charge of the war party saw the expression of astonishment that crossed my features.
But, luckily, he did not identify my expression as one
of recognition: had he done so I would have been
hard put to explain how a warrior of the Black Legion
could have known a Ganatolian swordmaster and a
Yathoon hordesman.

Instead, he misinterpreted my surprise as mere star-
tlement at seeing a Yathoon warrior in the city of the
Ku Thad. For while the various human races of Thanator frequently take service in alien cities, and while
it is not at all rare to encounter a Perushtarian trades-
man in Zanadar, a Ganatolian warrior serving in the
ranks of the Chac Yuul, or a Ku Thad dwelling in
Ganatol, the great, solemn-faced, stalk-limbed arthropods of the Horde stay with their own kind and are
not ever found in service with the forces of the human
nations of this world.

Proud of his capture, the squat, bandy-legged little
komad grinned hugely, hooked his thumbs in his gir-

dle, and nodded at the two silent prisoners.

"Fresh bodies for the Games, eh, friend?" he chuckled. "The Warlord will be pleased with them. Why, we
have not taken a *capok** prisoner in years. 'Twill be a
pleasure to see this one stand against a yathrib for the
Nuptial Games. I have always wanted to see one of
them in action with those ungainly whip-swords of
theirs."

I had gained control of my features by now and
permitted them to register slight curiosity.

"Aye, true enough, *komad*," I said indifferently. It
came to me suddenly that, in honor of the marriage of
Prince Vaspian and Darloona, the Chac Yuul would
hold one of their bloody gladitorial festivals in the
great arena of the palace compound that very afternoon. My blood ran cold at the thought. How could I
free my friends, while attempting to save Darloona
from the arms of the Son of Arkola? I did not think it
possible to accomplish both; and yet I could hardly
abandon Koja and Lukor to so horrible a fate as death
in the arena. Both had saved my life ere this, at the
hazard of their own.

"You are the *komad* Jandar, are you not?" the little
officer inquired. "I believe I have seen you in Prince
Vaspian's retinue ere now."

I nodded, and he identified himself as one Loguar,
an officer in the fourth cohort of the Legion.

"Where did you get these two?" I asked, with what
I hoped would sound like idle curiosity. Loguar was
happy to swagger his triumph and needed no spur to
his loquacity.

"Caught them in the lower city," he said, meaning
the slums of Shondakor, a dilapidated area of old tene-

---

* *Capok* is a rude colloquialism for the Yathoon insectoids. It
can bluntly be translated as "bug," or so Captain Dark notes
in the first manuscript of narrative of his adventures, the book
which I have edited for publication under the title *Jandar of
Callisto*, and to which the present book is a sequel.—L.C.

ments down by the river docks. "Sneaking along in the shadows, they were, and up to no good, that was obvious. The old one put up a terrific battle, for all his white hair. A devil with the sword, that one! Five of my lads will be months in the mending, and three others will fight for the Legion never again, for they are gone to Gordrimator."

By this, Loguar meant they had been killed, or so I surmise. Oddly enough, for a barbaric world of walled cities and tribal monarchs, the various nations of Thanator have only the most rudimentary kind of a religion. They worship a pantheon of divinities called "The Lords of Gordrimator," by which name they term the planet Jupiter, to which this world of Thanator is the fifth satellite; but the word "worship" may be too strong, for never yet have I met with a priest of this religion or nor have I seen anything that could be described as a cathedral or a temple.

Indeed, the only priest of any description I have heard of on Thanator is that inscrutable little being, Ool the Uncanny, and he is more wizard or enchanter than priest. But I had vaguely heard of the Thanatorian belief that the souls or spirits of the warrior dead travel to Gordrimator, which seems to be envisioned as a sort of paradise or afterlife, so I understood what he meant.

"Odd to see a Yathoon hordesman in the city," I commented. "Where are you taking them, if I may ask?"

"To the Pits," shrugged Loguar, meaning the dungeons beneath the royal citadel. "There they will be safe and secure until the Games."

"Very good. Doubtless someone will wish to question them as to their reasons for being in the city?"

He grunted and spat. "The Warlord generally questions prisoners, but on this day of days I doubt he would be interested. Well, I must be off with my prizes." He grinned, and tossed me a companionable

salute. Then he strode off into the palace with his war
party and the two captives.

I stood aside as they went past me, and as tall gaunt
Koja went by he clacked out one word in his harsh
metallic tones.

"*Horaj,*" he said.

He spoke in a low voice and I doubt if any heard
him, or if they did, they paid him no notice. The more
ignorant of the humans of Thanator, among which the
Chac Yuul must certainly be numbered, consider the
great stalking warriors of the Yathoon Horde as little
more than monsters, and certainly they do not count
them as intelligent beings on a par with mankind.
Hence if any of the members of Loguar's war party
heard the single word which Koja enunciated, they
put it down to a bestial grunting. But I have dwelled
in the war camps of the Horde and I know that while
the arthropods are degraded and cruel and belong to
the lowest rung of civilization, being merely nomad
warrior clans devoid of the nobler sentiments and im-
mune to the beauties of the arts, they are nonetheless
as fully intelligent as men.

What did Koja mean by that single word *horaj,*
which he doubtless spoke for my ears alone? *Horaj*
means "urgent."

By this enigmatic term, did he mean to communicate that he possessed vital information for my ears
alone? I could put no other construction on his remark. And surely Koja and Lukor had not run the
risk of entering the city of Shondakor for any other
reason than to communicate with me.

I paused in the entranceway for a few moments, in-
decisively.

The forced marriage of Darloona was but hours
away. And if Valkar and I were to attempt any sort of
rescue, we must lay our plans at once. And even now
he awaited my coming in our wineshop rendezvous.

But I must forgo that meeting, for all its urgency.

I turned on my heel and reentered the palace.

Despite the fact that time was running out, I could not delay having speech with Koja and Lukor. Some mission of overwhelming importance had caused them to dare the risk of entering the city of the Ku Thad.

And I must find out what it was.

BOOK FOUR

THE BOOK OF OOL

CHAPTER THIRTEEN

AT SWORD'S POINT

The Pits lay beneath the lowest levels of the palace, and although I had never had cause to visit them during my tenure in the service of Prince Vaspian, I was well enough aware of their location to find them without difficulty.

Getting in to see Koja and the gallant old Swordmaster would be another problem. But it seemed likely that my rank as a member of the retinue of the Prince would be sufficient to get me past the guards.

If it did not work, well, frankly, I did not know what I should do. If the secret network of passages within the palace walls continued into the depths of the dungeons, I was not aware of the fact. And I had no time to go exploring. Time, as I have already observed, was running out; and to employ yet another cliché, matters were coming swiftly to a head.

I had a hunch that the masquerade was about over. My imposture had escaped detection up to now, and my false history had survived scrutiny. But things were moving too fast for me now, and, as my reader will observe, I was beginning to take risky chances. I had no valid reasons to be in the Pits at all, and if queried by Vaspian or Arkola, I would not be able to satisfactorily explain my curiosity regarding these prisoners. But my friends were in danger, and that justified my taking even the most enormous chances—I was willing to risk even the disclosure of my true identity—willing even to jeopardize my entire mission.

I could do no less for those who had done so much for me.

And thus I descended into the Pits.

Luckily for me, they were not heavily guarded. Since the entire palace was in the hands of the Chac Yuul, how could an enemy of the Chac Yuul penetrate to this place? Such, at least, was the thinking that had decreed the Pits need not be heavily guarded. Were it not so, I could not have gotten as far as I did before a guard confronted me.

Down a long stone corridor I went, striding rapidly, my cloak tossed back from my right shoulder so that it would not impede the use of my right arm, my fingers brushing the pommel of my rapier.

Grim walls of rough stone lay about me; the air was chill and dank, and it reeked of the fetor of men held in long imprisonment with but the rudest of sanitary facilities.

What light there was, and there was but little, came from oil-soaked torches of black jaruka wood clamped with brackets of rust-eaten iron against the moldering stone masonry. These crude attempts at illumination cast a wavering orange glare and painted huge black shadows upon the walls. To me it seemed momentarily unreal. All of this scene through which I moved was like a movie set; I felt that I myself was unreal, a mere actor playing a role in some historical epic; even my garments, cloak and buskins and the slim rapier that slapped against my bare thigh with every step, added to this feeling of unreality.

Suddenly I turned a corner and found myself facing a large and nearly empty room paved with stone which was bestrewn with moldy straw.

In one corner of this large open area stood a rough wooden table, its top surface marked with rings of dried wine and ale, hacked with knives, as if generations of bored and idle guards had carved their initials upon it. A bucket of water and a dipper stood beneath the table, and upon it stood a candelabra of brass with three guttering candles. A wooden stool was drawn up to this table, and sprawled dozing thereon a burly guard could be seen. Only one guard! That was a stroke of fortune.

Opening off this large room were several cells. I could not, at first glance, tell what persons were immured within, for the shadows were deep and thick. But even if my friends were not imprisoned in one of these cells, it seemed likely that the dozing guard could tell me where they were being held.

The guard—his head was turned away from me, resting on his folded arms, so that I could not see his face—was a *komad*, as I could tell from the emblems clipped to the shoulders of his leather tunic. In other words, he was of the same rank as myself. This meant I could not use my position as a superior officer to bid him answer my queries; but my favored place in the retinue of the Crown Prince of the Black Legion would doubtless suffice to wring cooperation from him, as few officers of the Chac Yuul would be so foolish as to willingly go against the wishes of the man who would, with luck, someday stand in the highest place of the Legion.

"Sleeping on duty, *komad?*" I asked sharply, as I entered the room. It seemed at the time a good idea to put the fellow in the wrong at the beginning; that it was not at all a wise notion became evident almost immediately.

He started away from his nap and raised his face to look at me, with apprehension and anger mingling in his expression. He was a coarse, crude-looking oaf, with fleshy, unshaven jowls and mean little piggish eyes—eyes which narrowed the moment they rested upon my features.

His snarled curse broke off as delighted recognition dawned upon him. A gloating smile crossed his coarse visage, and my heart sank into my boots, for I had recognized him almost in the same instant, and I knew

I should get no cooperation from this particular officer.

For it was Bluto, the swaggering bully I had beaten
and humiliated at the city gate when first I entered
the walls of Shondakor!

Silently, I cursed my vile luck. Of all the officers in
the Black Legion who might have been assigned to
this particular post at this particular hour, it had to be
the one man in all the Legion least likely to cooperate
with my wishes.

"And if I am, what is it to you, little man," he
grunted, rising to his feet and laying one huge hairy
hand on the pommel of his cutlass. "What be your
business here, and where be your authorization?"

I have stated earlier in this narrative that this hulking brute was one of the biggest men I have ever
faced, and it was truly so. He was a colossus, towering
above me almost as much as Koja did. He was not in
the best of fighting trim, for a swag-belly hung over
his girdle and there was soft flab in his jowls and upper arms, and he looked somewhat the worse for
drink. But the rest of him was solid beef and he had
the advantage on me as far as weight and reach went.
He would make a dangerous opponent.

I touched the medallion of precious metal on my
baldric, the insignia which denoted me as a member
of the court of Prince Vaspian.

"Here is all the authority I need to examine a prisoner, *komad*," I said levelly. "I want a look at the two
strangers who were brought down here within the
hour. You know the ones, the *capok* and the white-
haired outlander in black. Loguar, a *komad* of the
fourth, brought them in."

He grinned nastily, eying me from his height.
"What do you want with them?"

I shrugged. "It is not what I want, Bluto, but what
the Prince my patron wants. They are to do battle in
the Nuptial Games following the royal wedding, and
he wishes me to see that they are in good shape for

fighting and have fed. If they are injured or have been mistreated, I am to inform him of the fact. Now, if you will be good enough to tell me where they are being held, I will be about my business—"

He lifted one great hand, stilling me.

"Bluto has his business, too," he growled. "Also his orders! No one gets in to see any prisoner without a note from the Lord of the Pits."

"But the Prince has expressly ordered—"

"*No one* gets past Bluto," he said heavily. And he drew his cutlass with a rasp of steel on worn leather, and held it ready in his hand, watching me from cold little eyes buried in rolls of unhealthy fat. A predatory expression crossed his face; he licked his thick lips with the tip of his tongue.

I stood there, struggling to think. Had the guard been any other except this bully, who hated me for making him look ridiculous in front of his men, I could perhaps have bluffed my way past him through the sheer weight of Prince Vaspian's name. But Bluto was happy to be able to refuse me what I wanted.

I could not, of course, go to the Lord of the Pits, as the officer in charge of the dungeon guards was called. He would be a senior officer and he would not be swayed by important names; he would want to see my authorization from the Prince in writing. And, even if I could bribe or bully the commandant into giving me a pass, there simply was no time. Minute by minute sped swiftly by, and every passing second brought the woman I loved closer and closer to a forced marriage with a smirking villain she loathed.

If I fought with Bluto, my false identity was exposed. For the duel might arouse guards housed nearby, and I ran the risk of being taken into custody as it was forbidden that Chac Yuul warriors fight among themselves. And how could I explain a corpse, if my skill with the blade were sufficient to strike Bluto down?

In this matter, as frequently in my past career, Fate

took the decision out of my hand entirely.

For Bluto lifted his blade and set its point against my heart. A leer of sadistic mirth distorted his coarse features and his voice was thick and hoarse with gloating menace.

"Bluto could kill you now," he growled, "and say you tried to force your way in. No one would ever know—"

I struck his blade aside with my arm.

"I am an officer of the Chac Yuui," I protested. "It would be an act of treason!"

He spat. "Treason, eh? You dirty little *horeb,* you call Bluto a traitor? You made Bluto look like a fool. You dared not face Bluto with steel. You fought with your hands, like a wench!"

I watched the red glare of fury in his cold little pit-eyes, and my heart sank. There was no hope for it— I must fight the man. I must duel here in the Pits, while every racing moment brought my beloved nearer to a horrible doom.

He was panting heavily now, working himself up to a berserk rage, as he had done that time I beat him at the gates. I tried to reason with him but there was no arguing with the man.

He roared out a string of filthy epithets and swung his great cutlass at my head.

I sprang backwards nimbly, avoiding the whistling blade.

He advanced, towering over me, growling curses.

There was no other way. I slid my blade free of the scabbard, and in the next instant we were at sword's point there in the black dungeons of Shondakor.

CHAPTER FOURTEEN

TO THE DEATH!

Barely did I manage to lift my sword to parry his blow. The impact jarred along the blade and numbed my arm. Bluto was immensely strong, and he had worked himself up into a bloodthirsty rage.

I backed away and let him come after me, snarling and spitting ugly curses, his face working. He swung at me, great lusty swipes, his heavy cutlass whistling through the air, and each blow I turned aside, but with great care, for his blade was much weightier than mine, and if I parried in such a way that the full force of his blow met my rapier squarely, he might snap my blade in two.

He fought like a madman, swearing wildly and hacking away with enormous energy. He had little or no science, but his giant strength and endurance, his superior weight and reach, were powerful advantages and for a time I was hard put to keep his edge from slashing my flesh.

As we fought, he taunted me.

"You—too proud to fight with Bluto at gate—too proud to face Bluto with sword, like a gentleman—use your hands on Bluto, will you, you filthy *horeb!* Now you fight Bluto, steel against steel—how do you like it?" he growled, his red eyes blazing with berserk fury, and whitish foam gathering at the corners of his mouth.

I saved my breath for the duel and did not deign to answer his foul-mouthed raving. I resolved to kill him as quickly as I could, but, as I soon discovered, it

is not all that easy to duel with a man who fights like
a maniac, swinging great blows with untiring strength.
So I continued backing away from his roundhouse
swing, while looking for an opening.

If I had been fighting an ordinary swordsman,
armed with a weapon similar to my own, I could have
killed him within minutes, if such had been my wish.
For I could have caught his blade and turned it aside
with a deft twist of the wrist, allowing my blade to
glide through his guard and my point to sink in his
breast. But Bluto was an entirely different sort of opponent, swinging wildly as if armed with a club, and I
continued to retreat warily before his advance, for if
any one of those blows had connected I would be
weaponless.

He began cursing at me to stand still and fight him
like a man, rather than to retreat like a coward. But I
paid no attention to his raving, watching his blade-
work for an opening.

Suddenly, one came—a wide swing that left his burly chest unguarded for a moment. This was the opportunity I had been hoping for and I lunged, my point
sinking into the fleshy part of his shoulder just above
the heart.

To my astonishment, it failed to stop him, or even
to slow him down!

He squealed like a stuck pig, but it was more from
blind rage than pain. And instantly he redoubled his
assault, whacking away with lusty blows which
knocked my blade from side to side like the slender
steel needle it was.

Obviously, his berserk fury was such that he was
virtually insensible to pain. It would take nothing less
than a direct thrust through the heart to fell the roar-
ing maniac.

Around and around the room we went, as I backed
away from his advance. The stone room rang like an
iron foundry with the clang of steel on steel. I felt my
way with caution, fearful of tripping over an unseen

obstacle, for I could not see what was behind me and I dared not turn my attention from Bluto for a second to snatch a glance over my shoulder.

I managed to pink him on the throat and on the upper arm, but these were mere slicing cuts, minor wounds, which gushed with blood and must have stung him but were not sufficient to disable him or even to slow him down.

By now he was streaming with blood and sweat, and foam slavered from his grinning jaws, but he still came on, showing no signs of exhaustion.

And then, very suddenly, the duel was over.

One wild, awkward blow had caught me unawares and my slim blade snapped off short, just beyond the hilt. A thrill of alarm ran through me as I realized I was now unarmed.

Murder flamed in his piggish little eyes and a triumphant note entered his hoarse, bestial howl as he raised his nicked cutlass for the kill.

Instead of jumping to one side, as he might have expected, I took a great risk—and sprang forward, to close with him!

Sometimes, in moments of great peril, when all seems utterly lost, it has been my experience that to do the completely unexpected can often snatch victory from between the slavering jaws of defeat. And never was this more ably proven than when I sprang into the embrace of the maddened colossus.

He was dumbfounded, caught with both arms and the heavy blade raised above his head, and as my body jammed against him he staggered off balance and fell stumbling to the rush-strewn stone pave.

And I was upon him like a striking jungle cat.

The broken sword hilt in my hand was all but useless. The blade had snapped off near the hilt, but where the steel blade had fractured was a sharp, jagged point.

This point I sank into the thick flesh of Bluto's neck —and ripped, tearing his throat out!

As I staggered, panting, to my feet, he died on the stone pave in a gush of reeking gore. To the last, an expression of blank astonishment filled his eyes with dazed incomprehension. I do not believe he understood that he was slain until his eyes glazed in death and his heaving breast gave one last shudder and was stilled forever.

I had not wanted to slay the poor fool, but he would have it so. A fight to the death, sword against sword, but it had been his death, after all.

I left him lying there in a pool of blood.

Taking up his sword in the place of my own, and borrowing the candelabra from the table, I set forth to search the Pits of Shondakor to find my friends.

It probably took no more than a few minutes, but in my state of anxiety it seemed like the better part of an hour. Even now, Darloona might be standing before the hideous idol of the Black Legion while Ool sealed her life forever to that of the oily weakling I once had served!

Most of the cells were empty, mere dim, noisome cubicles which bore a rude wooden bench and a heap of moldy straw. But some were tenanted—by the dead.

I paced swiftly down the first corridor, pausing before each cell and lifting my candelabra to illuminate the dark recesses within, before striding on.

Repulsive, naked *horebs*—the verminous rodents of Thanator, which sometimes attain the size of small dogs—fled wriggling and squealing from the light. One glance at that which served them for a banquet and I hastily averted my eyes, as nausea clutched at my throat.

But ere very much time had elapsed the flickering illumination of the candles showed a welcome sight— Lukor, looking pale and disheveled, chained to one wall of a filthy cubicle, and gaunt, solemn-faced old

Koja blinking his great black eyes, chained to the other.

"Ho! Jandar, is it you?" the old Swordmaster chortled with delight. "My boy, never have these eyes looked upon a more welcome sight!"

I had prudently taken a ring of keys from Bluto's girdle, and after a little fumbling I found the right one, unlocked the cell door and went in to relieve my comrades of their chains.

"I'm glad I could get here before you were interrogated," I said as I helped them remove their shackles. "Are either of you hurt? The Legion sometimes plays mighty rough."

Lukor sniffed, straightening his sober raiment and smoothing his small white beard into something resembling its customary neatness.

"Not at all, my boy, not at all! Oh, there was a trifle of a flurry before we were disarmed, but Koja there dispatched a few of the bandy-legged little wretches with his blade and I gave a couple of the others a brief lesson in swordplay; but neither of us sustained anything more serious than a few scratches," he said complacently.

Koja blinked his huge eyes solemnly at me as I unfastened his chains.

"It is good to see you again, Jandar," he said in his monotonous voice. I clapped him affectionately on the upper thorax and said I was happy to see him, too.

"But what in the world are you two fools thinking of, trying to get into Shondakor like this? Didn't you know you'd be spotted and seized before you got halfway?" I demanded.

Lukor sobered. "We had to do it, lad. Word of the Princess Darloona's impending nuptials to this Black Legion princeling leaked out and the Ku Thad got wind of it. Your friend, Marud, I fear, was responsible for that!"

My pulses quickened.

"Marud—the innkeeper? You mean he got through after all—with my message about the secret tunnel under the river and the city walls?"

Lukor looked surprised.

"Of course," he said. "How did you think Koja and I got inside Shondakor, if not by the hidden tunnel of which your letter apprised Lord Yarrak?"

I had not really thought things out. I guess I had assumed that Koja and Lukor had somehow sought to gain entry through the city gates and were taken prisoner. But now this surprising news changed everything. Marud must have been seized by the warriors of Ool the Uncanny on his way back into the city, instead of on his way out. I had not been sure which had been the case, but for some reason or other I had assumed he had been seized en route to the *entrance* of the tunnel.

I thought rapidly.

"Then this means the Ku Thad warriors are ready to attempt to retake the city by means of the underground passage?"

"That is true, and they are growing restive!" said Lukor, his merry eyes going grim. "Koja and I begged them to wait for some further news from you before charging into the middle of things, but the thought that their beloved Princess was being forced to wed the Prince of the Chac Yuul has maddened them to the point of throwing off all restraints. They will wait no longer, so we came on ahead, desperately hoping to locate you and to gain some word of your own plans in time to coordinate them with the attack of the Ku Thad. Jandar—Jandar! Why in the name of the Lords of Gordrimator did you never communicate with us again, after that first message?"

"It was impossible," I said. "The only man I could trust was the fat innkeeper, Marud—and the guards seized him as he was reentering Shondakor after delivering that first note from me. They were planning to interrogate him, probably under torture, for I am certain that Arkola the Warlord would not scruple over the matter of a little pain!"

"And did they? Get anything out of Marud, I mean?" Lukor asked. I shook my head somberly.

"There was a real man behind that fat belly and that foolish face," I said softly. "For he killed himself rather than yield my name to those who were to interrogate him."

Lukor cleared his throat.

"A very gallant gentleman," he said quietly. "I shall be proud to drink to his memory, when there is a drop of wine and a bit of leisure. But now—"

"But now we must get out of here—and fast, for every moment counts! Darloona will be wed to Arkola's son this very day—almost at any moment! We must get swords and do what we can do to interrupt the ceremonies."

And I cursed the low technology of the Thanatorians that they had not yet invented the wristwatch. For I had lost all sense of time by now and would have given my left hand to know what was the hour.

Koja gathered up the loose length of chain and passed it thoughtfully through his many-jointed, clawlike fingers, swinging it to assess the weight.

"As for Koja," he said, blinking owlishly, "he shall require no weapon but this heavy length of iron chain, for the small blades used by the members of your race do not fit his hand. But this length of chain will serve well enough."

"Then let us be going!"

Lukor led the way out of the cell, peering about through the dimness.

"Which way?" he inquired. I jerked my thumb toward the square stone room where Bluto's corpse lay in a puddle of congealing gore. We sprinted off down the corridor, our footsteps raising echoes.

"Is this not foolhardy?" Koja asked, thudding along at my side, his ungainly strides carrying him along at a rapid pace. "How can such as we hope to traverse the palace unmolested? Surely the first Chac Yuul warrior to spy us will raise the alarm."

"There is a network of secret passages hidden within the walls," I said. "We can travel far by means of them, and without being discovered. There should be a panel leading into the labyrinth of hidden passages in the hall beyond the entrance to the Pits—"

And then a pang of despair ripped through my heart! For even above the noise of our running feet and over the thudding of my own heartbeat, I could faintly hear a distant bell tolling the hour!

And Darloona was being married—*right now!*

"But—" Koja began. I cut him off with a curt word.

"Save your breath for running," I panted, and we raced down the echoing hall and burst into the stone room.

And stopped short!

Eyeing the corpse, old Lukor voiced a snort of laughter.

"I see you had time for a bit of practice ere coming to seek us out, my boy!"

I did not reply. I hefted the heavy cutlass in my hands and wondered what the next few moments would bring.

For there in the doorway that led to this chamber from the upper level stood a fat, smiling little man with gleaming, amused eyes.

"I told you that we would have another little talk, O Jandar," the man said in a high, breathy voice.

It was Ool the Uncanny.

CHAPTER FIFTEEN

IN THE HALL OF HOOM

These things I, Jandar, did not see happen, for I was
not there. But much later, when all was over, the fighting was ended, and Darloona taken from me, I heard
how they had chanced to occur. And I tell them to you
now, just as I heard them from the lips of Valkar,
Prince of the Ku Thad.

Valkar waited long in the wineshop, but Jandar did
not come. Minute by minute, time ticked past, the
hour appointed for their rendezvous came and went,
and still there was no sign of Jandar.

What had happened to prevent their meeting?
Valkar grimly counted over the possibilities, and none
of them were pleasant ones. Jandar's imposture might
have been discovered—his true identity revealed—his
mission of rescue unveiled.

If this were so, every passing moment might bring
danger closer to Valkar. For the *komor* well knew
how pain can wring truth from the lips of even the
bravest and most stubborn of men. Every minute he
remained waiting here in the tavern might draw their
plans closer to the brink of disaster. Even now, a con-
tingent of guards might be clanking through the
streets of Shondakor, bound for this inn.

The longer he waited here, the more likely was the
chance that he would be arrested.

At length it was so close to the time of the marriage
ceremony that Valkar dared wait no longer for his
friend. If Jandar had not come by now, he was not

coming. Some unforeseen happening had occurred to
shatter their plan. The gnawing unease, the feeling
that something had gone wrong, grew stronger.

Abruptly, Valkar rose from the wine-stained table,
tossed a glittering coin at the sallow-faced innkeeper,
and strode out of the wineshop, peering up towards
the towers of the royal palace where it rose beside the
plaza in the heart of the great city.

It was up to Valkar to come to the aid of his princess *and he must do it alone.*

Valkar had entered the palace and its maze of hidden passages within the walls only a few times before,
and always by the dark of night, when few were
abroad and the chances of being seen were slender.

Never before had he dared to enter the closely
guarded citadel by broad light of day. And, under ordinary circumstances, he would never think of making the attempt with the palace crowded with warriors
and officers, every corridor thronged with wedding
guests, a thousand scurrying servants making last-
minute preparations for the impending royal nuptials.

Under such circumstances, the chances of discovery
were vastly greater. However, Valkar had no alterna-
tive but to try it. For within the hour, unless he found
some means of intervening and bearing off the Princess to safety, Darloona would be married before the
hideous stone idol of the Chac Yuul devil-god, Hoom.

Under his cloak, Valkar was dressed in his most resplendent decorations, for this was a festival day and
all the chieftains of the Black Legion had been commanded to clothe themselves in all their finery as if
for parade.

Tossing aside his cloak, Valkar found it not difficult
to mingle with the other officers thronged before a
side gate, and to enter in their midst. His decorations
and ornaments were no less glittering than their own,
and thus he gained entry into the palace without detection or even being noticed.

Striding through the hallways, he thanked the mysterious Lords of Gordrimator for this small stroke of fortune! On previous secret visits to the palace of the Kings of Shondakor, he had entered the walls by a small door in the outer circuit of the walls, a door concealed behind a heavy growth of shrubbery. But in the broad light of day it was impossible to use that route without being seen.

Now that he was actually within the palace, he must find one of the sliding panels that would give him entry into the hidden passageways behind the thick walls. And this he found most difficult.

The trouble was, simply, that the palace was bustling with guests and visitors. Every room and corridor he passed, every rotunda and antechamber, was filled with people. On the rare nights when he had visited Darloona in secret to urge her to permit him to assist her in an escape, he had chosen a late hour when certain side passages were untenanted. Now, every passage was filled with busy people. Perspiration started on his brow; he had the horrible feeling one experiences sometimes in a nightmare, of racing against the clock, of struggling to avert some hideous doom, and of finding that every step is slowed and encumbered by an unseen impediment, so that one battles forward in slow motion while doom races nearer with every madly ticking second!

Straining to keep the tension from being visible on his features, Valkar turned aside and ascended a staircase to the second level, hoping to find a momentarily empty suite wherein to make his entrance through one of the hidden panels.

At last, after an agonized eternity of strolling past crowded rooms, he found a chamber empty of all occupants and wasted no time in striding to a further wall covered with a richly brocaded wall hanging.

The swordsman stepped behind the hanging and in a moment his searching gaze found one of the minute

and unnoticeable signs that marked a hidden door.
In another moment his fingers had found and depressed a secret spring.

With a faint clashing of hidden counterweights, the
door slid open and a black hole yawned before him.
Without hesitation he stepped within and sealed the
panel shut behind him.

He had brought no candle or lantern into the dark
maze of passageways, for it would have looked odd
for an officer to be strolling through the brightly lit
palace carrying a lantern when it was broad daylight.
And it took his eyes a few moments to adjust to the
dimness.

But ere long he could see well enough to make his
way down the narrow passage to a side branch where
coded markings would direct him to his easiest route.
Valkar had spent many hours studying the code
wherewith the secret labyrinth was marked, and he
could find his way through the winding maze with
ease.

It was quite different here inside the secret passages
by day. By night the narrow tunnels are drenched in
impenetrable gloom, and without a candle or some
other means of illumination it is almost impossible to
find your way. But during the daylight hours a sufficient amount of light leaks into the passages through
cracks and crannies in the walls to spread a dim,
vague illuminance by which, if one goes with care,
one can make one's way without great difficulty.

Before long Valkar found the right passage and followed it to its end, striding as swiftly as he dared in
the half-gloom.

He came at length to a spyhole and slid its covering
aside to peer through the small aperture at a scene of
astounding magnificence.

The temple of the devil-god of the Chac Yuul lay
before him.

Before the conquest by the Black Legion, the Ku

Thad had used the immense hall for a throne room. But now a hideous stone idol stood on the topmost tier of a vast flight of low, broad marble steps where once the Kings of Shondakor had sat in state.

The idol was very old, black with age, and grimy with the stain of splattered blood—for the horror of human sacrifice was not unknown to the savage warriors of the Black Legion.*

Half again as tall as a man, the stone image squatted atop the uppermost tier, its legs folded tailor-fashion beneath it, its bulging paunch sagging down in an obscene fashion.

Five arms the idol lifted to its sides and each claw-like stone hand grasped a weapon of war. As for the sixth hand, it was empty, and held out over the top

---

* To this passage in Chapter 15 Captain Dark has attached a footnote to the effect that this is the only god, or near-god, he had ever encountered in all his wanderings and adventures upon the face of the jungle world.

Elsewhere, in this volume and in *Jandar of Callisto*, its predecessor, he has mentioned on occasion the puzzling absence of any formal or hierarchical religion among the various nations of Thanator. It would seem natural, from an anthropological point of view, for the barbaric peoples of Callisto—who, with the single exception of the Sky Pirates of Zanadar, seem to belong to a level of civilization approximating that of our own Bronze Age—to have elevated a pantheon of savage divinities comparable to those of the Greeks, the Romans, the ancient Egyptians, or the old Norse. But, oddly enough, such does not seem to have been the case. Save for a nebulous and never-defined reverence for "the Lords of Gordrimator," (Jupiter), the Thanatorians seem to worship no gods, seem to have nothing in the way of a priesthood or a system of temples and shrines. It is all very odd.

Save for this monstrous idol, Hoom, and Ool his wizard priest, no other divinities or their priestly servants are mentioned in the two volumes of Captain Dark's narrative. Hoom may well have been an import, for in the next chapter we shall learn something of the origins and background of Ool the Uncanny, and it may well be that the little wizard-priest introduced the idol of his far-off and mysterious homeland when he entered among the ranks of the Black Legion. Such, at least, is my conjecture.—L.C.

steps as if clutching for human prey.

The face of the god Hoom was indescribably hideous, screwed into a leer of malice, with glaring eyes under scowling brows, and bared fangs. Curling horns sprouted from its bald pate, between the sharp, pointed ears.

A grisly necklace of human skulls dangled about its thick throat.

Such was the demon-god of the Chac Yuul.

Such was the grim divinity whereof Ool the Uncanny was high priest!

On the broad steps below the place where black Hoom squatted, leering and monstrous like some bloated and gigantic toad, a glittering assembly awaited the coming of the priest.

Arkola was there, magnificent in black velvet, his strong face grim and unsmiling. There, too, were the lords of the council and the high chieftains of the horde, in their barbaric finery.

Light streamed through tall tapering windows to flash in mirror-polished shields and burnished helms, to twinkle from the jewels in sword hilt and girdle and the gems that flashed about the throats of the Chac Yuul women.

A step or two below the idol stood Darloona. She was superb in a long gown of golden satin sprinkled with small diamonds, but for all her beauty and the splendor of her gown, Valkar could see the tension and fear in her pale, set features, and in the way her hands gripped and twisted at a small scrap of handkerchief.

Vaspian smirked and lolled at her side, resplendent in silken robes, a gilt coronet upon his brows. From time to time he leaned to whisper in Darloona's ear, and at the way her face tightened with distaste, Valkar could guess the message of his leering whisper, and his hand gripped his sword hilt until the knuckles whitened.

The bell had long since rung the hour, but it seemed that this splendid company yet awaited the coming of Ool. A murmur arose from the throng, as the Chac Yuul whispered. What was keeping the fat little wizard-priest?

Valkar, from his hidden place, searched the audience with a narrow gaze, but not for Ool the Uncanny. He wondered if Jandar was in the crowd, and although he searched for him carefully, he saw him not. For the hundredth time, he wondered what calamity could have prevented his comrade from attending their vital meeting.

Now a stir and rustle went through the throng.

Valkar peered about and saw that at last Ool the Uncanny had entered the hall. The fat little man was muffled in thick robes of a dull, drab hue, and the cowl of that robe was drawn, concealing his face. Head down, hands tucked into his capacious sleeves, the little wizard stumbled across the top of the flight of steps from an entrance on the far side. He was aware of his lateness and had hurried, for he was breathing heavily. Valkar wondered what could have detained him—and again wondered what had become of Jandar.

Now Ool descended the topmost steps to stand between the Prince and the Princess, with the great stone idol towering up behind him.

And now Valkar could delay no longer. With or without Jandar he must act swiftly now, before the nuptials were sealed and Darloona was wed to the man she loathed.

Valkar touched the hidden spring and the panel slid aside.

With a leap he attained the dais whereupon the idol stood. Ripping out his sword, the Prince sprang down the steps, catching a swift glance at the expression of astonishment that crossed the faces of Prince Vaspian and Darloona at his unexpected appearance. Ool still had his back turned and saw nothing.

Daylight flashed on the blade of his rapier as Valkar lifted the sword and sent its point hurtling to cut down Ool from behind before he could speak the doom-fraught words which would seal the marriage.

Ool turned and looked Valkar directly in the eyes! And Darloona *screamed!*

CHAPTER SIXTEEN

THE MIND WIZARD OF KUUR

Cold chills went down my back as I stared at the fat little wizard-priest who lounged in the doorway of the Pits.

"What are you doing here?" I blurted. It was an inane thing to say and it made him laugh, a thin, titter of malicious humor that had no mirth in it.

"Why, I am here for our long-delayed little talk," he purred, slitted eyes agleam with mischief. "I told you we would speak together at a later time—and this is it."

He paused, surveying the corpse that lay sprawled in congealing gore amidst the tumbled rushes. His eyes lifted to the bare cutlass I held, and again that mirthless titter fell from his fat smiling lips.

"You are a man of action, I see, O Jandar! Alas, you would not lift cold steel against a fat old man, who hath naught wherewith to defend himself?" The purring voice trailed off on a questioning note. I hefted the heavy sword, feeling foolish. Koja and Lukor were watching all this without comprehension.

For some reason the fat little priest gave me pause. I should have simply run by him, but for some reason which I cannot quite explain this seemed not the thing to do. It was, I think, a matter of *presence*.

Whatever else he may have been, Ool the Uncanny was not a man you could easily ignore!

Now he came waddling into the square stone room, hands tucked within capacious sleeves. He wore his usual thick robes of drab hue. His sandals slapped and whispered against the stone pave.

His sharp glance took in the tall somber arthropod and the keen-eyed, white-headed little Swordmaster behind me.

"A warrior lord of the Yathoon people, and a master-swordsman from the City in the Clouds," mused Ool thoughtfully. "How in the name of thirty devils could an ordinary mercenary from Soraba know such as these—so much that he commits mutiny, aye, and murder, too, in the freeing of them! 'Tis a puzzle, indeed: a mystery . . . there is much about you, O Jandar, that savors of the mysterious."

Lukor cleared his throat, a little impatient bark of sound.

"I believe you said something about a bell, lad? Why do we stand here talking, when the lass is about to wed that fool of a Prince?" he demanded.

I opened my mouth to speak, but Ool said swiftly: "Rest easy on that point, O Lukor of Ganatol; the Princess Darloona cannot be wed until I arrive in the Hall of Hoom beyond the Throne Chamber. I know, for 'tis I, old fat Ool, who will conduct the nuptials."

"How do you know me, priest?" snapped Lukor. Ool smiled lazily and his eyes drifted from one of us to the other.

"I know you at least as well as you know yourself, O Swordmaster—and the *komor* Koja of the Yathoon Horde—and you, as well, O Jandar of—what should I say? 'Tellus' or 'Terra'—or 'Earth'? Aye, Jandar of Tellus—that would be the proper construction."

Jandar of Tellus!

Shock ripped through me, the shock of complete amazement, as I realized this placid little butter-colored Buddha somehow knew my closely guarded secret—knew that I was not native to this world of Thanator, but was a visitor from a far-distant planet! *But how could he have known that?*

Almost as if he read the question in my mind, he smiled again, obviously enjoying my mystification.

"I know many things, O Jandar, which are hidden from other men. You, and all those that dwell within the walls of Shondakor, think me but a priest of Hoom, my god—that, or a wizard of strange gifts and stranger wisdom. You have seen me many times, and each time it has entered your mind that my flesh is yellow and my black eyes aslant, and that I am unlike any people you have yet encountered upon the face of Thanator—but never has it occurred to you to think about this puzzle."

Ool spoke truth. Suddenly it came to me that I knew well the races of Thanator: the Ku Thad of Shondakor, with their amber skin, emerald eyes, and flaming manes—the papery-white Sky Pirates of Zanadar, with their lank black hair—the bald-headed, crimson-skinned men of the Bright Empire of Perushtar—the Chac Yuul warriors, with their greasy, swarthy skins and colorless hair—and those crossbreeds, such as the Ganatolians. *And not one of these races had the butter-yellow skin and slant black eyes of Ool the Uncanny!*

Yet *never* had I noticed this!

"And for very good reasons, O Jandar of Tellus," the fat priest chuckled. "I am one of the Mind Wizards of Kuur, dark shadowy Kuur that lies beyond Dragon River amid the Peaks of Harangzar, *on the other side of Thanator.** My people share a curious science, a mental discipline that permits us to read the thoughts and minds of other beings. As you can well imagine, this art gives us an unusual advantage over the other races of Thanator, an advantage we are not hesitant to employ."

---

* As pointed out in *Jandar of Callisto,* Jandar's knowledge of the world of Thanator is limited to the same hemisphere wherein he first materialized. Neither he nor any of the Thanatorians with whom he has become friendly has any knowledge of the other side of the planet, which is why he was able at various times to pretend his homeland lay on the other side without risking exposure.—L.C.

"*That's* how you led the Chac Yuul into Shondakor!" I cried.

"Of course," he chuckled. "An archivist possessed knowledge of the secret tunnel beneath the river and the outer walls, and thus I gained ascendancy over Arkola and a place in his councils, by bartering the secret of a safe road into the Golden City for—*power.*"

A cold flash of reptilian greed shone momentarily in his slitted eyes.

"We are a small, a dying race; but we have a mighty power over the minds of other men, a power which, if used adroitly, can lay an empire within our reach. I found my way into the inner councils of the Chac Yuul by means of my mind power, and the Chac Yuul seized a kingdom. That iron man of war, bold Arkola, thinks he rules the Black Legion, but it is *I* am the master here!"

"Then using your mind power, you were able to still suspicion of your race in the brain of every man you met?" Lukor asked keenly. "That is why it never occurred to anyone to wonder who and what you were, with your yellow skin and slant gaze?"

His bald pate nodded sleepily.

"True, Ganatolian. It is but the least of my abilities. When this gallant warrior here came into Shondakor, I knew him from the very first as a man from another world. His is a strange tale, and it will have a stranger ending, as I somehow seem to know—"

"Know you aught of the mysterious power that guided me to this world?" I cried, for the mystery of my coming hence had long plagued me. Reluctantly, Ool shook his head and his cold eyes were dull and opaque.

"Nay. There are things hidden even from the probing skills of a Mind Wizard: but someday you will know the answer—if you live." He smiled.

"From the first, I knew of your true identity and of your cause and mission," he said sleekly, animation returning to his keen gaze. "I did not reveal you to my lords, for it amused me to see you play this little drama out to its end. But that end has come, aye, the last act is upon us even now, and I fear me you shall none of you live out the scene to its final curtain."

I lifted my cutlass into view.

"Have you forgotten, Mind Wizard, that I bear cold steel and you are unarmed?" I said tensely. His smile was mild and bland.

"And would you strike down an old man in cold blood?" he murmured. I shrugged.

"I will kill any man who stands between me and the woman I love," I growled. "I have naught against you, Ool; naught have you done to oppose me in my quest, therefore I am willing to let you live. Only do not get in my way—"

"Alas for your quest, O Jandar, it is not my will that you rescue the Princess of your heart," he smiled.

"You mean—"

"I mean that for all these months I have been working towards a certain end," he replied, and I knew then that I would have to kill him.

"What end, Mind Wizard?" I asked.

"I am not here by chance or accident, but by plan. We of dark Kuur must subjugate this hemisphere, and since we are few, we must set nation against nation, weakening them through endless wars, so that we may carry off the victory in the end. According to the decision of my Masters, the Prince of the Chac Yuul weds the Princess of Shondakor, thus provoking war between the Sky Pirates and the Black Legion. Out of that war, one victor shall arise—and we of shadowy Kuur shall dominate that victor. Alas, our plans have no room in them for Jandar of Tellus, or Koja of the Yathoon Horde, or Lukor of Ganatol—or even for the Ku Thad."

Suddenly I saw everything, clear and plain as if it were written on the wall.

It was the meddling little Mind Wizard had set

Prince Vaspian and his father at odds, had cast the seeds of suspicion into their minds, each of the other. For surely, if the mind wizardry of Ool the Uncanny could blot a question of his race from the minds of those he met, that same grim art could *insert* a thought into the minds of others just as easily.

A sense of futility arose within me. All that we had striven for, all our plans and hazards, had been but as a game played out for the amusement of this fat, sinister little priest!

He had known when I despatched poor brave doomed Marud to the Lord Yarrak with my letter which revealed the secret tunnel under the walls and the river. That was true—now I remembered!—it had been *Ool's men* who caught Marud on his return!

But why on his return? Why let him get to the warriors hiding in the Grand Kumala at all, when Ool could just as well have seized him ere he entered the secret passage? Why let him pass the letter to the Ku Thad, unless—

—Unless the Golden Warriors were walking into a trap!

"You are not stupid, O Jandar," the little Mind Wizard chuckled. "Indeed the mighty Yarrak and his gallant warriors will find themselves entrapped when they come through the tunnel this day and gamble all on one last, brave attempt to reconquer Shondakor! For I shall alert a full cohort of the Legion to wait hidden by the secret entrance of the tunnel, and as they emerge into the streets of Shondakor, they shall face the last battle and the doom of all their kind."

Grimly I stepped in front of him and set the point of my sword over his heart.

"You have just signed your own death warrant, wizard!" I said.

His cold, clever eyes probed deeply into mine, and his gaze was not worried but placid and serene and smiling.

"Think you I am a fool, O Jandar of Tellus?" he said softly. "Think you I came here to explain everything, to put myself into your power, without a means of escape? I am not a fool, Earthling; nay, 'tis you who art the fool. You should thrust home with that clumsy sword, and speak after. *Now it is too late.*"

And then a thunderbolt struck me directly between the eyes and I fell forward into a sea of black gloom.

Agony lanced through my skull as I swam groggily back to consciousness again. I could feel the gritty stone flags against my cheek, and the dank odor of musty straw was heavy in my nostrils.

Blearily I opened my eyes and strove to see what was happening.

Behind me, Koja and Lukor lay crumpled on the stone pave. Ool had struck them down even as I had been felled by his mental bolt. The power to read and to manipulate minds must include with it the strange and awful skill to employ the mind as a weapon. Ool's trained mind was able to project a stunning mental blow before which any lesser mind was helpless.

Why, then, had my own unconsciousness been but a momentary thing? Why did I rouse to wakefulness, while Lukor and Koja lay sprawled in the grip of an eerie mental paralysis?

Perhaps the answer lay in my own nature. I was not native to this jungle moon of Thanator; my body, my brain, had evolved upon a far-off planet. The bolt of mental force which the fat little Mind Wizard of Kuur had projected had stunned, but had not thrust me down into full unconsciousness. Perhaps the intensity of that stunning bolt had been attuned to the frequence of minds native to Thanator. Perhaps Ool the Uncanny had, for a moment, forgotten my extra-Thanatorian origin. It was a small thing to forget— doubtless, it had seemed of no great importance. But it seemed, after all, that the fate of a world hung on that little error he had committed in his complacence.

I resolved that he would feel the full weight of that error *now!*

Springing to my feet, snatching up the cutlass where it had fallen from my hand as I fell, I faced Ool, who had been bending over Lukor and who now started around with amazement written all over his placid, buttery features.

My brain throbbed abominably—I had the great-grandfather of all headaches—but I grimly thrust the consciousness of pain from me and sprang upon him, sword in hand.

From under his voluminous robes, Ool drew a rapier. So he was armed after all! His pretense at being unarmed was just another deception—just one more lie. It would benefit him little: I had learned the art of the blade from Lukor himself, and he was one of the greatest masters of that art on all Thanator. The fat little man could not long stand against my flashing steel, and now he knew his mental bolts had but a momentary and passing influence on my alien intelligence.

We fought without words, the little Mind Wizard and I, with no one to watch. Our only audience consisted of a dead man and two unconscious warriors.

It was a strange duel. In many ways, it was the strangest battle that I have ever fought.

Ool knew hardly anything of swordplay; his soft, plump hands were not accustomed to the grip of a sword hilt. Nor was he used to violent physical exercise. In no time his fat jowls and bald brow glistened with the sheen of perspiration and his breath came in panting gasps and his arms trembled from weariness and exertion.

But Ool could read my mind, and he knew in advance where I would direct every thrust and stroke— and his blade was there ahead of me!

It was an odd sensation. In a way it was like fighting yourself, like battling against a mirror image, pitting your blade against an adversary who knew precisely every move you would make even before you made it!

A cold horror gripped me. I had faced powerful swordsmen ere now; it was absurd to feel qualms of dread, crossing steel with this fat, puffing little priest. But so much depended on the outcome of this duel that my mind was a dizzy turmoil of fear and tension. Koja and Lukor lay helpless, mentally paralyzed by the bolt of uncanny mind force: if Ool slew me, my helpless friends would follow me down to Death's amazing kingdom. The woman I loved would be forced into the arms of a sneering coward, the gallant warriors of Lord Yarrak would walk directly into a trap, the small, peaceful kingdoms and cities of Thanator, cities I had never seen, would fall to the cunning of the Mind Wizards—*a world lay helplessly in bondage if I were slain!*

I wonder if ever before, in all the history of Thanator or of any other world, so much rested on the outcome of a single duel. The fate of a world, the destiny of many nations, depended on my quick thinking, steady hand, and flashing sword!

I tried to fence automatically, without conscious thought, relying on the sheer force of training and instinct alone, hoping in that way to overcome the advantage Ool's unearthly mind power had over me. Alas, it was in vain: whatever the nature and extent of his telepathic skills, he continued to anticipate, by a fraction of a second, my every thrust, parry, and stroke.

Perhaps his mental probe went deeper than I even guessed. Perhaps he could read me clear to the depths of my unconscious and could scrutinize those fighting instincts, those trained responses, on which I now relied. Perhaps he was alert to those tiny triggering impulses of nervous energy as they set into action the twitching of my muscles, long ere those muscles moved in actuality. I know not. I only know that wherever my point flashed, the flat of his blade was there.

Only the Lords of Gordrimator know what would have been the eventual outcome of this weird battle of strength and steel against mind magic.

Perhaps my very superior endurance would have won out in the end, or perhaps Ool's strange powers would have gained the ascendancy in the duel, and he would have struck at me, using some tactic of advanced swordsmanship drawn from my own brain to strike me down.

At any rate, it was not my hand that slew him, but the hand of a dead man that struck his doom.

As I advanced, plying my blade in a glittering dance of death, the little wizard retreated, shuffling along backwards. Around the huge square stone chamber we went . . . and then the hand of Fate struck.

The corpse of Bluto lay where I had struck it down. A puddle of cooling gore splashed the rushes. His dead limbs lay asprawl, and as Ool shuffled backwards, retreating from my point, he struck the dead hand of Bluto with one foot, staggered off balance, and fell over backwards, striking his bald pate on the cold stone pave.

His skull split like a ripe melon . . . and thus the weird duel of sword skill against mind magic came to an end, and death came to Ool the Uncanny at the hand of a corpse!

BOOK FIVE

THE BOOK OF DARLOONA

CHAPTER SEVENTEEN

THE FALL OF HOOM

As Valkar sprang down the steps of the high altar and drew back his arm to plunge his blade directly into the back of the robed and hooded little wizard-priest, Ool turned and looked him full in the face, and Valkar gasped, and paled, and his blade went wavering to one side.

"*Jandar!*" he cried in astonishment.

Was it relief—or joy—or amazement—that flared in the emerald eyes of Darloona?

"Jandar—?" she echoed wonderingly.

At her side, Prince Vaspian blanched, and turned an incredulous gaze on the hooded figure who stood a few steps above him.

"Jandar!" he gasped bewilderedly.

I laughed and threw back my hood, tossing the heavy robes aside, and stood above them, grinning with reckless humor, the heavy cutlass in my hand.

For, of course, it was I who had emerged from the far side of the Hall of Hoom, muffled in the thick robes I had taken from the corpse of Ool the Uncanny who lay dead in the Pits of Shondakor. Hunched over so that I seemed no taller than the fat little Mind Wizard, shuffling along in imitation of his waddling stride, I had gained a place close to Darloona without a single person in all that mighty hall guessing my identity. But the rasp of Valkar's buskin against the stone step had made me turn—just in time to let him see and recognize my face under the shadowing cowl, and turn his blade aside before it drank my heart's blood.

After Ool fell and split his skull, ending our uncanny battle in the Pits, the spell which had subjugated my comrades, Lukor and Koja, was broken. Donning Ool's robes as a handy disguise, I had swiftly found the nearest entrance to the maze of secret passages that lay within the walls of the royal palace, and we made our way to the Hall of Hoom where I knew Darloona was to be found.

Prince Vaspian saw the look in my eyes and the naked sword in my hand, and realized suddenly that this was the end of an imposture. His lips curled in a sullen snarl, and he tore his rapier from its jeweled scabbard, but I disarmed him with a practiced twist of the wrist and he fled from me, abandoning the Princess.

"Jandar—is it really you?" she whispered as I put my arm about her shoulders and turned to hold the astounded throng at bay.

"It is I, my princess," I replied calmly. "Think you that Jandar would not move heaven and earth to protect you from the arms of that weakling? Fear not for your helpless people—Vaspian will not very long be in a position to harm them!"

Valkar spoke from behind us in a clear, penetrating voice.

"Jandar entered the city pretending to be a mercenary and won a place in the ranks of the Black Legion in order to rescue you, my princess," he said. "His daring and courage, his cool head and quick mind, have saved you from a hideous parody of a marriage! Now you must come with us, swiftly, without argument—"

But just then we had no time for talk. Arkola, his face a savage mask of ferocity and rage, thundered a command at his bewildered guards who came charging up the stair towards where we stood. Valkar and I met them with flashing steel and drove them back a pace.

Darloona, however, would not obey our wishes and

retreat to the top of the altar level where it was safer. The brave girl snatched up the rapier the cowardly Vaspian had let fall in his ignominious flight and stood beside us, adding the strength of her blade to our own.

Within seconds, four guards lay gasping out their life on the bloody steps and we had won a moment's respite from the assault.

But a hundred stout warriors of the Black Legion thronged the hall in a guard of honor and Arkola thundered commands that snapped them from their paralysis and sent them charging up the flight of marble steps in a massed body.

Our swords flickered and played like summer lightning, and men fell screaming, splashed with gore, but others came charging over the flopping bodies of the fallen, and we were hard pressed and retreated, step by step, holding our own only by advantage of superior height, as we stood higher on the stair than did they who sought to assault us.

Still, it was only a matter of time before sheer weight of numbers dragged us down. As I fought, I wondered desperately—where were Koja and Lukor? They had hidden in the antechamber as I went out to impersonate Ool and seize the Princess, but surely they had heard all the commotion by now and knew we were fighting for our very lives here on the steps below the altar of Hoom!

I dispatched an opponent and turned to see if Darloona was safe.

She was not only safe, but fighting like a tigress. How glorious she looked, her red-gold hair streaming about her lithe body like a tattered war banner, the fire of battle shining in her splendid green eyes, her full red lips parted with the excitement of the moment. In a second her flickering blade cut down the warrior she had engaged and she turned her enigmatic gaze on me.

"This is all madness, Jandar—yet, well met! I had

not thought that we should ever meet again, save perhaps in the spirit, when our souls should travel on that long journey to stand before the tall thrones of the Lords of Gordrimator," she said.

"I could not desert you, my princess," I said.

"It was very brave of you to seek me out amidst the legions of the Chac Yuul," she said somberly. "Yet now all my plans are ruined, and my people are doomed—"

"I could not stand idly by and see you wed to a man you loathed!" I protested. She shook her head fiercely.

"But I must! Else my people will suffer!"

"Let us await the outcome of this day," I suggested. "For I managed to get word to your uncle, Lord Yarrak, of a secret tunnel beneath the Ajand and the city walls, and ere long the Ku Thad will enter Shondakor in force, and mayhap your people and not the Black Legion will be the masters here before this day ends."

Hope flared suddenly within her glorious emerald eyes, and her warm full lips parted breathlessly as if to speak—but then they were upon us in strength again, and we were both too busy for further conversation just then.

They pressed us hard, ringing us about with flashing steel, and although we fought magnificently, I knew in my heart that it was but a matter of time before superior weight of numbers would crush us down.

Yet it was not in me to complain of my lot. For indeed, were I to fall here, I could not think of a better way to die than this—battling for my life beside the woman I loved, a sword in my hand, grim laughter on my lips, Darloona beside me!

We fought on, but without hope. . . .

Suddenly the warrior whose sword I had engaged fell back a step, dropped his point, and cried out in fear. His features paled and his mouth sagged open, and his eyes went beyond me and froze as if fixed on some fearful apparition which stood behind my back.

"The god—*moves*," he cried with horror.

The other warriors about us staggered back from us now, their gaze transfixed with terror on something behind us.

"The god—*lives!*"

Risking a sword between the shoulders, I turned swiftly and cast a swift glance behind me. What I saw made me start with astonishment!

Above us on the flat dais stood the hideous stone idol of Hoom, devil-god of the Chac Yuul. Very horrible was Hoom, with glaring eyes, pot belly, leering fanged jaws gaped wide in a gloating grin, monstrous arms spread as if to crush us puny mortals in his multiple embrace.

And Hoom . . . *moved!*

Even as I stared in amazement, the arm which was extended out over the stairs *lifted* into a position of command!

And a deep, hollow voice boomed out, filling the great hall with rolling echoes!

"LET THEM GO FREE," it thundered.

Swords wavered and fell; men stared up with expressions of utter astonishment frozen upon their pallid features.

I sprang into action. I knew not what had caused this weird and inexplicable phenomenon, but I seized the opportunity for escape which it held out to us. Valkar and Darloona stood, gripped in the same amazement that held the others petrified. I signaled them frantically.

"Come! The panel—*now,* while we have the chance!"

We sprang up the steps to the dais, and Vaspian saw us.

He was no less the superstitious savage than his fellows, but jealousy and suspicion colored his mind. His features distorted into a vicious snarl as he saw us eluding his vengeance, and he came leaping up the stair after us, sword lifted for the kill.

But it was Hoom who slew!

The great stone arm that was lifted in a commanding position came smashing down—and crushed his skull. Vaspian fell dead on the steps of the high altar in a welter of splattering gore, and the room erupted into fury!

"Kill them all!" Arkola thundered, waving his great blade. A host of swordsmen sprang howling on our heels.

I darted around behind the idol, and found a stone door open in its back. Within, his hands working a series of levers, sat Lukor, his merry eyes dancing with delighted mischief—and Koja, whose deep metallic voice, through a wooden trumpet arranged so that the words seemed to come from the very mouth of the idol, had supplied the booming command.

In a flash the entire mystery was revealed. The image was hollow and a simple system of weights and counterweights enabled whoever sat within to move the idol's arms up and down through slots and grooves. Doubtless this was the secret of Ool's authority over the Black Legion—he struck at them through their superstitious terrors of the unknown.

I learned later that Koja and Lukor had lurked in concealment, awaiting my return, until the sounds of the uproar caused by my unmasking alerted them to peril. They had hurried out to a new position of concealment behind the idol, and by accident had touched the secret spring that opened the hidden door in the idol's back. The discovery had offered them a more powerful method of assisting us than merely adding their swords to our own. But now the imposture was over, and half a hundred warriors were charging up the stairs to pull us down. I thought swiftly. If the massive stone idol were hollow instead of solid, then it was not as heavy and immobile as it looked—

"Here—with me!" I said curtly, and I set my shoulder against the back of the idol and—*heaved!*

Valkar, Koja, and Lukor grasped my plan instantly, and lent their strength to my own while Darloona stood, hands pressed to her heart in an agony of suspense.

Would our desperate scheme work? There was no time to think of an alternate. I clenched my jaw and threw the full weight of back, arms, and shoulders into one last terrific effort.

And Hoom—moved.

The idol shuddered, slid forward on its dais with a grating of stone against stone, struck the horns of the altar, and toppled over!

Men were crushed beneath its ponderous weight, for even though Hoom was hollow, still he was fashioned of massive stone. The monstrous idol came sliding and crashing down the steps, spilling men to either side, squeaking and crunching over the buckling stair. Then it crashed full length and went rolling down the steps like some colossal juggernaut of destruction. The multiple stone arms broke away; fragments of stone went flying to every side; I saw one mammoth stone hand spin away and smash a fleeing warrior to bloody ruin, for all the world as a man might crush a fly with the palm of his hand. Dozens were crushed to death; scores were maimed or injured.

Midway down the stair, Hoom struck an obstruction and shattered. His grinning head cracked and broke off and went skipping horribly down the steps, straight for the place where Arkola stood, his strong face frozen in a mask of incredulous horror.

The head smashed full into him and skidded on, leaving him a broken, dying thing.

Thus died Arkola the Usurper.

CHAPTER EIGHTEEN

THE CONQUEST OF SHONDAKOR

We saw no more of Hoom's murderous fall, for we seized the opportunity afforded by his juggernaut-like passage down the stone stair to duck into the secret panel from which Valkar had sprung.

I seized Darloona's arm and thrust her ahead of me, with Valkar going before and Koja and Lukor at my heels. We ran through dark passageways and it seemed, from the uproar, that the entire palace was filled with the clamor of battle. Had the Ku Thad struck at last? We came out onto a broad and level terrace overlooking the city and gazed with delight upon what we saw.

Down every street came yelling mobs of Shondakorians, brandishing clubs, sticks, tools—whatever they could lay their hands on.

Before them, scattered units of the Black Legion retreated in confusion. And in a moment we saw the reason why—for there, in the forefront of the howling mobs, battled the warrior nobles of the Ku Thad with mighty Yarrak in the fore, his beard blowing on the wind, his great sword catching dayfire as it rose and fell tirelessly, smashing down warrior after warrior of the Chac Yuul.

In truth, the Ku Thad had come at the best possible moment, and half the city was theirs!

I laughed, weeping with delight, shaking Valkar's shoulder, yelling and pointing. Darloona's eyes shone with fierce, queenly pride and her lips trembled. Koja and Lukor recognized the bold warrior lords of the

Golden People and shouted with joy and triumph.

But there was much fighting to do before the city was truly ours, for the Black Legion, although taken by surprise, still vastly outnumbered Darloona's warriors, and although the populace of the city had recognized Lord Yarrak and had risen in arms to join the battle for their beloved princess, they were poorly armed and could not stand up to Arkola's trained and disciplined troops. Even as we watched, the progress of the loyalists slowed to a crawl as Chac Yuul units sped to reinforce their sagging lines.

Then the inexplicable intervened.

A dense black shadow fell over the embattled streets below and before any could look up in surprise a deafening explosion and a blinding flash of flame erupted in the very midst of the thickly packed Chac Yuul warriors.

Another explosion—and another! We stared up to see the skies filled with fantastic flying vessels which had appeared over the embattled city as if by magic.

It was the Sky Pirates of Zanadar, and they had launched their long-impending attack against the Black Legion at last!

The ungainly flying contraptions of the City in the Clouds were like great wooden galleons, made fantastical with carven poop, fluttering banners, ornamental balustrades. They hung aloft on immense, slowly beating wings, buoyed up against the pull of gravity by the powerful lifting force of the mysterious gas wherewith their hollow double hulls were suffused.

To the eye of the uninitiated, the sky ships of Zanadar were a thrilling and unbelievable sight, a fleet of enormous galleons that rode the golden vapors of Thanator's skies as the galleons of another world might ride the blue waves of the sea. But Lukor, Koja, and I had labored at the wheels of similar vessels but months before, and we knew the ingenious system of weights and pulleys that manipulated those vast un-

gainly wings, and the unique structure of the flying
galleons which were made of compressed paper instead of wood, and thus weighed only a fraction of
what their ocean-going counterparts on another world
would have. Still and all, they were an incredible
achievement, and had it not been for the rapacious
greed and cruelty of the Sky Pirates, who used their
aerial armada to prey off the merchant caravans of
weaker peoples, I could have applauded their amazing
skills with undimmed enthusiasm.

Nothing on my world had ever equaled the fantastic achievement of the Zanadarians, although that
mighty genius of the Renaissance, the immortal Leo-
nardo da Vinci, had sketched out plans for just such
wing-powered ornithopters in his secret notebooks.
And had he had access to the powerful lifting gas
wherewith the Zanadarians nullified the weight of their
flying ships, and had he also possessed the secret of
the strong, molded, and laminated paper construction,
the skies of old Earth might well have seen such a flying navy as this, half a thousand years before the triumph at Kitty Hawk.

Never before had I seen the ornithopters of Zanadar
actually engaged in battle; now I saw the immense
tactical advantage the fantastic flying galleons of the
Sky Pirates possessed over land armies, and a qualm
went over me. Unless some unexpected disaster intervened to demolish the imperial ambitions of Prince
Thuton of Zanadar, his aerial navy could conquer all
of Thanator and subjugate her peoples with ease.

Indeed, the Sky Pirates of Zanadar formed, if anything, a far greater menace to the peaceful nations of
this jungle world than did the Mind Wizards of Kuur,
who were few in number and who lacked military
might.

Hovering on their slowly beating vans, the ponderous flying machines hung against the golden skies like

something in one of the nightmarish paintings of
Hieronymus Bosch or Hannes Bok. Far above the
reach of spear, arrow, or catapult they hovered, and
from the safe vantage of their height they rained down
explosive missiles on the crowd-thronged streets below.

It was the hated Chac Yuul they were attacking,
luckily for us, and the fire bombs wreaked a terrible
toll of the beleaguered Black Legion warriors. Before
my gaze the defensive lines about the palace were
crumbling and the victorious ranks of the Ku Thad
pressed forward, beating back the broken and demoralized forces of the foe.

Ere long, it seemed likely that the surviving Chac
Yuul warriors would take refuge within the palace itself, which was constructed on the lines of a fortress,
and which could be held indefinitely against siege. It
was needful, then, for me to carry word to Lord Yarrak concerning the secret entrance into the palace—
the hidden route whereby Valkar had often found his
way into the network of secret passageways and thus
to the suite of the Princess Darloona. For unless Yarrak made swift use of this secret door, he would ex-
haust his strength in a costly and time-consuming
siege of the palace.

There was no time to lose.

I seized Valkar's arm and swiftly drew him aside,
suggesting that he withdraw to a secluded corner of
the terrace and guard the safety of the Princess, while
Koja, Lukor, and I sought to fight our way through the
battling mobs to the side of Lord Yarrak.

Valkar protested that there was no reason why he
should remain behind in security while we risked all,
but I had no leisure in which to argue the point and
tersely said so.

"Take care, Jandar," the Princess begged. I made no
reply, but after one long look into her emerald eyes
and a brief salute, I turned away and swung out over

the balustrade of the terrace and began clambering down the outer wall of the palace, followed by Koja and Lukor.

Obviously, it would have wasted much time for us to have attempted to work our way out of the palace through the mazelike network of secret passages. This route was much shorter and swifter. It was also, of course, much more hazardous: but I had faced a thousand perils in the service of my princess ere now, and I was not likely to flinch from one more danger.

Fortunately the outer wall of the palace was encrusted with elaborate sculptures. I have noted before the considerable similarity between the architectural style of Shondakor and the fantastical stone structures of the enigmatic ruined cities of Cambodia, such as Angkor Vat and Arangkôr. The surface of the walls was covered with enormous stone masks which stared down like so many carven gods on the embattled streets below. Stone devils and dragons, gargoyles and gorgons, leered and laughed from between the calm features of graven divinity, and their profusion of horns and beaks and claws afforded us a broad choice of handholds and toeholds wherewith to clamber down the two stories to the street level below. Thus without any particular difficulty we reached the broad plaza before the main gate of the palace.

I found that matters had gone in the very direction I had assumed they might, and that the main forces of the Chac Yuul had already retreated into the palace, while small groups of surviving Black Legion warriors sought similar refuge in one or another of the stone buildings of the city. From these citadels they were fighting a twofold battle against the Ku Thad in the streets and the Zanadarians aloft in the skies.

Arkola had erected a rude defense against the impending attack of the Sky Pirates during the last days of his regime. Rooftop catapults had been set in readiness to do battle against the flying machines of Thuton, and as I gained the ground at last I saw to

my surprise that the embattled Chac Yuul warriors
had actually managed to bring down at least one of
the great aerial galleons.

A well-placed stone missile, hurled with terrific force
from one of these rooftop war engines, had smashed
the control cupola of this galley, and grappling irons,
securely hooked into the ornamental carvings, figure-
head, and deck balustrade, had drawn it against the
roof of a nearby building, from which bonds it was not
likely to escape. Even as I gazed the Chac Yuul archers swept the decks of the captive ornithopter with a
deadly rain of arrows, and thus the flying armada of
Zanadar was lessened by at least one vessel.

But now Chac Yuul warriors, fleeing in broken rout
before the victorious advance of the Ku Thad, were all
about me, and I had no time to observe further events.
For I was busy fighting for my life against the panick-
ing warriors.

With Koja at my left hand and gallant old Lukor at
my right, we formed a flying wedge and cut our way
through the fleeing rabble to the forefront of the ad-
vancing Ku Thad. We three made a magnificent team,
and the terror-stricken Chac Yuul melted out of our
path, helpless to oppose us for long.

It was a scene of strange and terrible beauty, apoca-
lyptic in its grandeur and destruction. The streets were
filled with battling men, and they rang with the steely
music of clashing swords, the shouts and war cries of
the victorious, the howls and shrieks of the injured
and the dying. Corpses lay all about, amidst the rubble
of shattered stone, and the air was darkened with a
pall of drifting smoke from burning buildings. The
heavens resounded with the deafening explosion of
the bombardment of the Sky Pirates, and their mighty
winged ships darkened the ground with their monstrous gliding shadows. All about me men were fighting, falling, fleeing. The day of vengeance had come at
last for the Black Legion, and the day of victory had
dawned for the brave warriors of Shondakor.

We fought on through a scene of nightmarish splendor and power, while all about us a dynasty died and a new age was born.

At length we recognized the grim features of Lord Yarrak as he fought at the forefront of his warrior nobles, his beard flying in the murk, his eyes ablaze with victory, his great sword rising and falling tirelessly as he cut down the squat, swarthy men who had long held his city in their merciless grip, and who now received no mercy from his avenging blade.

He knew me at a glance, and his eyes lit with amazement to see me here in the streets amid the struggling hosts. Swiftly I drew him aside and satisfied his apprehensions, assuring him that Darloona was in a place of safety, guarded by his own valiant son, for which he gave heartfelt thanks to the Lords of Gordrimator.

"But as you can observe," I said tersely, "most of the surviving Black Legion warriors have already retreated within the walls of the palace, from which vantage they can safely hold the gates against a thousand warriors, while picking off your men with well-placed archers."

"That is true, Jandar," he nodded in grim assent.

"There is, however, a secret entrance into the palace, which was discovered by your own son, Prince Valkar," I informed him. "If you will follow me, we can be within the palace before the Chac Yuul are aware of it, and can open the gates to the body of your warriors."

"Lead on, then!"

Summoning a small band of picked swordsmen to accompany him, Lord Yarrak, Lukor, Koja, and I swiftly made our way to the secret door whose hidden place Valkar had disclosed to me many days before. I do not think that a single eye marked our progress, for the bombardment of the Zanadarian flying machines had set afire several nearby buildings in their efforts to destroy the rooftop catapults which imperiled the safety of the aerial fleet, and the drifting smoke of the conflagration effectively hid us from view as we crept along the outer wall of the royal citadel to the small stand of ornamental sorad trees whose thick dark foliage concealed the secret door from discovery.

My fingers fumbled along the rough stone of the wall and within but moments they had found and depressed the secret spring. A mighty slab of stone sank soundlessly into the earth, revealing the black mouth of a secret passage which yawned before us. With a reassuring word to Lord Yarrak and his nobles, I stepped forward without hesitation into the throat of the hidden passageway and within moments we had vanished from sight. The stone slab rose behind us and once again became part of the walls of the citadel.

It would be to no particular purpose to bore my reader—if any eye but mine own shall ever peruse these pages—with a lengthy and complete account of the battle which ensued.

Suffice it to say that, once we had breached the walls of the palace by means of the hidden entrance, our flashing swords swiftly cut down the astonished guards the Chac Yuul leaders had set over the palace gates, and it was but the work of moments to remove the massive bolts which had been set in place to hold the gate secure against the entry of the Ku Thad.

And once the gates were opened, and the victorious forces of Lord Yarrak poured within, the palace fell to us without a prolonged and costly battle. For, although those of the Chac Yuul who survived sought to blockade the hallways and corridors, and to make us pay dearly in the lives of our warriors for every advance, they were helpless to oppose us for long. Yet once again, I thanked whatever gods might be that I had spent so many weary hours in the exploration of the secret passages within the massive walls of the palace. For by means of this network of hidden

ways, I was able to circumvent every attempt by the
Black Legion to block our progress. Each time they
sought to seal off a corridor or close a suite of apartments against us, I simply sought and found a hidden
panel in the walls and led a force of Ku Thad warriors
through the labyrinthine maze, coming out *behind* the
barricade to strike down the surprised Chac Yuul who
guarded it.

In this manner we very swiftly invested the entire
palace from top to bottom, slaying a vast number of
the Black Legion, and taking captive those whose
prudence or cowardice was sufficient to overcome their
stubborn sense of superiority and who laid down their
weapons and surrendered to our advance.

The battle had taken hours and it was now late afternoon. But—save for a few scattered pockets of resistance, where a handful of Black Legion warriors
still held out and refused to surrender—before night-
fall the Golden City of Shondakor was conquered and
the victorious Ku Thad reigned again in the mighty
metropolis of their ancestors there on the shores of the
river Ajand.

CHAPTER NINETEEN

VICTORY—AND DEFEAT!

The weeks that have passed since the conquest of Shondakor and the victory of the Ku Thad and the destruction of the Black Legion have been quiet, but not exactly restful, for we have labored long and mightily to repair the damage wrought by the great battle and to bring into some semblance of order the chaos and confusion into which Shondakor fell during the struggle among the three forces.

The bombardment of the Sky Pirates of Zanadar was actually less destructive than it seemed at the time, for the main goal of Prince Thuton was obviously to crush the Black Legion rather than to level the city of the Ku Thad. Thus most of the fire bombs had been directed at mobs of Chac Yuul warriors in the streets, and only those buildings which housed the rooftop catapults had been assaulted by the Sky Pirates. Only a few buildings had suffered any extensive damage from the aerial bombardment; and since by far the greater number of structures towards the heart of the city, in the area around the royal palace, were built of stone, the fires caused by the Zanadarian bombs had not spread.

It had, of course, crossed my mind at the time that we might succeed in destroying the Black Legion only to find ourselves locked in battle against the Sky Pirates. Fortunately this did not prove to be the case. In fact, even while we were still engaged in crushing the vast vestiges of Chac Yuul resistance within the royal palace, the bombardment ceased—the armada lifted

—the Sky Pirates suspended their attack upon Shondakor and rose into the upper air, wheeling slowly above
the city, with the obvious intention of sailing off to
their distant stronghold, the City in the Clouds.

This cessation of the attack, this withdrawal of the
vast flying contraptions from the skies over Shondakor, was most puzzling. At the time I could not account for it. It was only later that the dread truth
burst upon my consciousness and I realized the ghastly reason that had occasioned this inexplicable retreat
of the Sky Pirates. . . .

The golden skies of Thanator darkened swiftly with
the advent of night, which falls swift and suddenly
upon this jungle world. Huge Imavad ascended the
skies, glowing against the dark like a vast rose-red
lamp. Tiny Juruvad, as the peoples of this world call
Amalthea, the innermost moon of the planet Jupiter,
was also aloft, a minute flake of golden fire. Ere long
the shimmering lime-green sphere of Orovad, or Io,
would soar up into the heights of heaven.

But before Orovad rose over the horizon, the city
was ours.

Great was the joy with which the citizens of Shondakor hailed the triumphant warriors of the Ku Thad.
Ten thousand voices rose up to chant the stately
measures of the anthem of the immemorial stone city
by the river Ajand. Surely the measured thunders of
that noble and ancient song were audible to the last of
the Sky Pirates of Zanadar as they sailed off down the
darkling sky, bound for their far-off mountaintop fortress amidst the mountains of Varan-Hkor which rise
hundreds of *korads* away, beyond the trackless jungles
of the Grand Kumala, on the borders of that unknown
and boreal wilderness called The Frozen Land.

I could almost think that the music of that mighty
anthem rang against the cold and watchful stars that
peer down in redundant remote scrutiny on the little

dramas played out by mortal men across the small stage of this little world.

More than one half of the Black Legion perished in the battle of Shondakor.

Arkola, the Warlord, and his son, Prince Vaspian, and many of the clan leaders and high commanders of the Black Legion died there in the Hall of Hoom, either crushed beneath the rolling juggernaut of their fallen devil-god, or slain by the swords of Valkar, Darloona, and myself, when we held the stair against their advance.

Leaderless, a milling chaos of confused and frightened men, under attack from every side, the common warriors of the Chac Yuul fell in their hundreds and their thousands before the mobs of angry citizens, the disciplined swords of the Ku Thad, or the rain of death and fire from the flying navy of Zanadar. Over a thousand were slain by Lord Yarrak's force within the palace itself.

The small number which remained of the once-mighty conquering bandit horde were broken and demoralized. They were disarmed and captured with little effort; many of them laid down their weapons and surrendered rather than continue the unequal struggle any longer.

Lord Yarrak could have had the captured remnants of the Chac Yuul slaughtered. It was no less than they deserved, and in this barbaric world, mercy was a rare phenomenon. However, the great Baron spared all those who had been taken; he expressed himself as being weary of killing, sick of slaughter, and as the few who had survived the destruction of the Legion could never again form a menace against the peaceful nations of Thanator, he set them free and drove them forth from the gates of Shondakor into perpetual exile, never again to return to the lands of the Ku Thad on peril of death.

Thus the Black Legion passed forever from the great stage of history; scattered bands of them infested the mountains for some little time, preying on merchant caravans, but these small bands dwindled and soon were heard of no more. Rarely has a more decisive and total victory been recorded in the annals of warfare.

In the weeks that followed I have set down this narrative account of my deeds and adventures on the moon Callisto, and now I am almost at the end of my story.

Lord Yarrak has promised me that when I have concluded this history, a band of his warriors will carry it from the gates of Shondakor through the jungles of the Grand Kumala to that enigmatic ring of monoliths which stand as eternal guardians over the Gate Between The Worlds. They will set the bundle of manuscript within the circle of the standing stones, and will watch as the cycle of the moons comes again to that hour when the mysterious sparkling beam of unknown force blazes forth once more to link this world of Thanator and my own Earth, the planet whereupon I was born, with its weird and inexplicable shining pathway.

And for the second time a bundle of manuscript that is a true narrative of my remarkable adventures upon the surface of this strange and terrible and beautiful world will dematerialize into a sparkling cloud of energy and go flashing up that weird ray to vanish from the knowledge of men in the dark places between the stars.

Will this record of my adventures find its way across the limitless void? Will it cross unharmed the vast distance of some three hundred and ninety million miles of space to rematerialize once more in the Lost City of Arangkôr amidst the trackless jungles of Cambodia, on the planet Earth?

I cannot know for certain.

I can only hope that this record of my discoveries and deeds will survive that mysterious trip through space, and come to the attention of some person of my own world. For I should not like to think that this account, wherein I have so laboriously preserved the lore of another world, will be lost forever in the darkness between the stars.

There is a curious blending of nostalgia and sorrow in my heart as I set down these last few words.

There is a restlessness in me, and a hunger to visit again the fair and splendid cities of my youth, to see dawn break crimson over the green jungles of the Amazon and the stars glimmer faintly in the clear gliding waters of the Oronoco, to drink raw gin in the fetid back alleys of Rio, and taste the indescribable savor of fresh black coffee and frying bacon on the cold winy air of a little camp high in the Rockies.

I would like to see the fabulous lights of Broadway beating up to dim the few faint stars above, and to see the mighty shaft of the Empire State lift its flashing crown of searchlights against the gloom, and to wash down a sizzling veal scallopini with a bottle of tangy Chianti in that Italian restaurant on Bleecker Street in crazy, cluttered Greenwich Village.

All of these things I would like to do, and all of them I could do, if I truly wished.

Yes, for I could accompany that band of hand-picked Ku Thad warriors across the jungles of the Grand Kumala to that ring of stones that marks the place where I first set foot on the surface of this world of Thanator.

Then I was naked as a babe, alone and friendless, lost in a weird and hostile world of savage men and hideous monsters.

Now I have a multitude of friends: somber Koja with his great eyes blazing like black jewels in the featureless casque of his gleaming, inhuman features;

gallant old Lukor, that chivalrous and gentlemanly
master swordsman; brave, noble Valkar and wise
Zastro and stern, kingly Lord Yarrak—good friends
and gallant comrades all, tried and true, and tested
in a thousand battles. They love me well, that I know,
and will stand beside me in peace or in war.

And, although they have heaped me with honors,
ennobled me with the high rank of a *komor* of the
Ku Thad, thus giving me a place in the lordly nobility
of Shondakor, and although I know that the Golden
people of the Golden City will be proud and pleased
to offer me a home amongst them for however long I
wish to stay . . . I also know that they would not
stand in my way if I should desire to make that long
trek through the jungle country of the Kumala and
stand naked amidst the standing stones of the Gate,
to bathe again in that shimmering force that will
whisk me across millions of miles of space to the
world that is my home.

My departure would grieve my Thanatorian friends
and my old comrades would miss me at their high
councils and on the ringing plains of war, we who
have so often stood shoulder to shoulder, a smile on
our lips, a sword in our hands, facing together the on-
slaught of our enemies.

They would mourn my departure, but they would
set no obstacle before it.

But of course I shall not enter the Gate Between The
Worlds.

It well may be that I shall never again stride the
shores of the Oronoco, the back alleys of Rio, or the
busy sidewalks of Broadway.

Perhaps, someday, I shall return, but not yet and
not now. For now Thanator is my home. Here on this
jungle world of war and battle and intrigue, I have
found good friends, a cause for which to fight, and a
woman to love.

Never shall I leave Callisto until she stands once
again at my side.

If that longed-for day ever comes, if she truly yet lives, if I have succeeded in rescuing Darloona from the clutches of her enemies—then and then only will I think of going home once more.

My days are busy, assisting my friends in the rebuilding of war-shaken Shondakor. My afternoons and evenings have been devoted to setting down, however crudely, with what poor skill I possess, this record of my experiences.

My nights are given over to—*dreams*.

And my dreams have a soft, generous scarlet mouth, a splendid and womanly figure, clear, tilted eyes of emerald flame, soft warm flesh of amber gold, and a savage mane of rippling, red-gold splendor, like a mighty war banner.

Never can I forget her heart-shaking beauty, her peerless courage, her strength and fierce pride.

Never shall I forget my last glimpse of Darloona. The joy and horror and heartbreak of that cataclysmic moment echoes yet within the depths of my being.

The palace was finally ours and the last dejected survivors of the overwhelmed and broken Chac Yuul were disarmed and bound, our helpless captives.

We raced through the corridors, Yarrak and Lukor and Koja and I, to the broad terrace where I had left Darloona under the protection of Valkar's sword. All about us lay scenes of carnage and devastation; corpses lay strewn about the hallways amidst the wreckage of broken barricades.

Bands of the Ku Thad paced vigilantly the hallways of their retaken citadel, herding groups of Black Legion captives before them or seeking out the last pockets of resistance. Swords were naked in their hands and the joyous light of victory shone in their weary faces.

At length we reached the level terrace and looked out over a city rejoicing in the first hour of its freedom. Here and there a building in flames cast a drifting pall

of black vapor across the skies, but the streets were
cleared now and the gold and crimson banners of imperial Shondakor shook out upon the night winds
their heraldic colors in token of victory.

Through the smoke-veiled skies the last few ornithopters yet circled the vast metropolis, ere rising to
the heights of the sky for their long return voyage to
Zanadar, the City in the Clouds. One mighty vessel
yet hovered close above the palace. I recognized it as
the *Kajazell*, the flagship of the aerial navy, Prince
Thuton's own ship.

We searched the broad terrace with eager eyes, but
strangely enough we did not see either Valkar or Darloona.

The ghostly chill of apprehension touched my
heart.

Then I heard a stifled cry from behind me. It was
Lord Yarrak, an expression of consternation on his
face. With a trembling hand he pointed to a crumpled
shape that lay huddled in the shadow of a mighty pil-
lar.

It was Valkar!

His eyes were closed, his limbs slack, and a thread
of scarlet fluid leaked from a great wound on his brow
to stain the deathlike pallor of his features.

My heart racing, I knelt beside his sprawled figure
and laid my palm against his breast. He yet lived, for
the throbbing of that vital organ beat however faintly
against my touch.

"Valkar! What has happened!" I cried as my comrades gathered about us and Lukor knelt to set a cup
of water from his canteen at the white lips of our injured friend.

His eyelids flickered and a trace of color came into
his marble cheeks.

"Jandar," he whispered hoarsely, and in so faint a
voice that I had to bend low to catch his next words.

"They sprang on me . . . from behind . . . three of

them I . . . slew . . . but there were . . . too many," he whispered feebly.

"And the Princess?" I cried in an agony of suspense. "What of the Princess? What of Darloona?"

"Seized . . . taken," he whispered, and then he spoke no more. The effort had drained what small reserves of energy his body retained, and he fell back in my arms unconscious, although not seriously injured.

"Taken!" Lord Yarrak repeated, horror written upon his stern and kingly features.

"But by whom?" Lukor asked, rendering vocal the question that throbbed in the hearts of each of us.

And then the answer came—in a woman's cry!

"Jandar! O Jandar!" came a faint, far voice. A voice that I knew. A voice that brought me swiftly to my feet, the sword ready in my hands.

"Darloona? Where are you?" I shouted, and the answer came, faintly as if from afar, "Here!"

And then I turned, and looked up, and saw her.

Her eyes looked longingly into mine; her warm lips were opened in a tremulous smile and her arms reached out as if to clasp me. My heart leapt within me, and her next words—the last words I was to hear from her lips—echo within me to this very hour, and shall remain in my memory so long as life endures: never had I dared to hope that I should hear her speak those words to me, and that I have heard them from her very lips is a precious memory which I shall shore up against whatever empty, lonely years of bitterness and despair lay ahead for me.

"O Jandar, my beloved, my gallant warrior—I love you! I love you! I shall love you until I die—"

A thunderous burst of emotion shook me to the core and rose to overpower me. I stood speechless, heart-shaken, basking in the glory of it—that my own hopeless and unspoken love was returned by my peerless and incomparable princess! *She loved me!*

My heart was too full for speech. But my eyes gazed deep into her own, and I doubt not that the eloquence of my gaze of longing and adoration communicated my feelings to her heart.

It was a magic moment, but already she was receding from me, her face dwindling, a pallid oval against the deepening dusk.

I stared after her, heartbreak and longing written on my anguished features. For as long as we remained within sight of each other, we continued to gaze deep into each other's eyes.

But it was not very long.

For, locked a helpless captive in the clutches of Prince Thuton, who grinned down at me with cold gloating triumph written in his cruel face, Darloona was swiftly borne away from me as she stood on the deck of the *Kajazell*, the flagship of the Zanadarian fleet, which rose from hovering above the terrace of the palace, circled us briefly once, and then rose again to fly at a vast height, dwindling down the sky, bound for Zanadar, the mountaintop fortress of the bold and powerful Sky Pirates of Callisto.

EDITOR'S NOTE

And it is at this point that Captain Dark's second narrative of his adventures on Thanator comes to an abrupt end.

In editing his manuscript for publication by Dell Books, I have striven to retain wherever possible his own precise phrasing. What changes I have made have been for the purpose of simplification. And, of course, wherever Captain Dark has inadvertently made an error in word usage or spelling, grammar or punctuation, I have corrected it.

It will be understood that, marooned as he is on the fifth moon of Jupiter, our author does not have easy access to a dictionary.

In concluding my version of this second volume at this point of tension and unresolved conflict, I wish I could assure my readers that the remainder of the story will yet be told. But this I cannot know for certain. It may be that this is the last word we shall ever receive from the first Earthman in history to explore the marvels and mysteries of that remote world. Or it may be that a third manuscript will materialize in that weird jade-lined well in the Lost City of Arangkôr in the unexplored jungles of Cambodia.

Only time will tell. . . .

LIN CARTER

A NOTE ON THE THANATORIAN LANGUAGE

Both in *Jandar of Callisto* and in this book which serves as its sequel, Captain Dark reveals a considerable amount of information about the language spoken on Thanator.

While he is not a trained linguist and does not convey language data in anything even roughly approximating a working vocabulary of the Thanatorian tongue, sufficient information is given in the course of his narrative to tell us quite a bit about the language. He himself comments on the unusual fact that the identical language is spoken by all the human and nonhuman races of the jungle moon, and that not only is no other language known upon Thanator but the very concept of "another" language is difficult for the Thanatorians to grasp. In this respect, I call to your attention the incident in *Jandar of Callisto*, Chapter 4, where Captain Dark describes the immense difficulties he had, not so much in learning the universal language of Thanator under the tutelage of Koja of the Yathoon Horde, but in getting across to the friendly arthropod the very fact that he did not know the language and required tutelage in it.

From what the two Callistan books reveal, it would seem that the common tongue of that world bears no relationship to any terrene language; at least, I have shown the following data on Thanatorian words to two language experts, Dr. Ralph Morton Jamieson of my old alma mater, Columbia University, and Professor Alton Ames of the Department of Languages of Brooklyn College. Both experts are willing to be quoted in saying that the Thanatorian vocabulary which follows does not seem allied to any of the terrene languages, as a comparison of cognate terms reveals. (Professor Ames thought it looked more like a derivative of Esperanto than anything else, but I am not familiar enough with that famous synthetic language to agree.) Both acknowledged that the language is obviously agglutinating, not unlike Turkish or Hungarian, but bears no other similarity to those languages.

I have prepared the following brief glossary from my study of the two manuscripts, and it follows.

LIN CARTER

A GLOSSARY OF THE THANATORIAN LANGUAGE

AKKA-KOMOR: seems to mean, literally, "high-chieftain"; and as far as Captain Dark informs us, the term is used only among the barbaric warriors of the Yathoon Horde.

AMATAR: possession, a prized but soulless "thing."

ARKON: among the Yathoon, at least, this seems to be the title of the supreme chieftain, perhaps cognate with "king." Captain Dark unfortunately does not give us the originals of the Thanatorian words he translates as "prince," "queen," or "king," so we cannot be certain this word is used by others besides the Yathoon, who in many respects have a separate vocabulary all their own.

BICE: a gold coin of considerable worth; beyond mention of the bice, Captain Dark reveals nothing of the coinage or currency of Thanator.

BORATH: a tall tree found in the jungle country of the Grand Kumala. Captain Dark mentions only two other forms of arboreal life on Thanator.

CAPOK: an impolite colloquialism by which the baser elements of the various human races of Thanator refer, derogatorily, to the Yathoon insectoids; cognate to "bug."

CHACA: the color "black."

CHAC YUUL, THE: Captain Dark translates this term as "Black Legion." A bandit horde under elective leadership, which Captain Dark likens to the Don Cossacks or the *condottieri* of the Italian Renaissance.

DELTAGAR: a monster of the Thanatorian jungles which Captain Dark describes as a twenty-foot super-tiger with scarlet fur and a lashing, whiplike tail edged with jagged serrations. It has enormous canines like those of a terrene sabertooth, two curling horns sprouting from the brow, and a ruff of coarse mane which stands up around the base of the skull. Captain Dark killed one in the arena of Zanadar (see *Jandar of Callisto,* Chapter 12).

GORDRA: the Thanatorian word for "eye." Note that it is possible this word is the plural; Captain Dark seems uncertain on this.

GORDRIMATOR: the name by which the Thanatorians call the planet we know as Jupiter. Conjecturally, I suggest that the name means *gordra ima tor* or "world of the red eye," so-called from the prominent feature called The Great Red Spot which has been noted by terrene astronomers. The gods of the Thanatorians are called "the Lords of Gordrimator," which suggests that the priesthood of Thanator (if such indeed exists, for Captain Dark's narratives thus far contain no reference to any such, save for the cunning little devil-worshipper Ool the Uncanny), in whatever religious doctrines they have evolved, teach that Jupiter is the home of their pantheon of gods. On this point, however, we can only conjecture; for Captain Dark himself frequently points out that he has learned precious little about the religious practices of the jungle moon.

HORAJ: the word wherewith Koja alerted Jandar to the importance of the news he carried, as described in Chapter 12 of the present book. The word means "urgent."

HOREB: a naked Thanatorian rodent of repulsive habits; the word is used in a derogatory sense much as we use the word "rat."

IMA: the color "red."

IMAVAD: the Thanatorian name for Ganymede, the fourth moon of Jupiter. Captain Dark explains that Ganymede appears rose-red from the surface of Thanator (Callisto), and he further notes that the name means, literally, *ima vad,* "Red Moon."

JARUKA: this seems to be one of the more common trees of the Thanatorian jungle country; Captain Dark describes it as having a gnarled black trunk and branches and weird scarlet foliage. No tree of this description is native to Earth, and a botanist whom I have queried points out that red foliage would preclude the existence of chlorophyll in the leaf structure, which makes it difficult to see how such a tree could live.

JURU: little or small.

JURUVAD: the name by which the Thanatorians refer to the moon Amalthea, the smallest and most inward of the Jovian satellites, visible from the surface of Thanator as a minute flake of golden fire. The name means "Little Moon."

KAJA: the sky.

KOMAD: a military rank which Captain Dark explains is inferior to that of a full chieftain; in other words, a subchieftain, or captain.

KOMOR: the military rank of "Chieftain." Superior to the rank which is equivalent to captain, it would seem to equate with major or colonel.

KORAD: a Thanatorian unit of distance which Captain Dark says is about the same as seven miles.

KUA: the color "golden," and perhaps the metal as well (?).

KU THAD, THE: the name by which the amber-skinned, flame-haired, green-eyed race dominant in Shondakor denote themselves. The term translates as "The Golden People."

LAJ: the Thanatorian word for "sea." Captain Dark's narratives describe two inland seas, or land-locked lakes, on Thanator; the larger of the two is known as Corund Laj and the smaller as Sanmur Laj.

LAJAZELL: a small winged reptile of which two distinct species exist on Thanator, the first inhabiting the desert regions (see ZELL), and the second, the shores of the inland seas. *Lajazell,* the lakeside species, Captain Dark aptly terms "seagulls."

OLO: a small knobbed wooden club worn at saddleside wherewith the Thanatorian mounted warriors keep their unruly mounts (see THAPTOR) under control.

ORO: the color "green."

OROVAD: the Thanatorian name for Io, the second moon of Jupiter. Captain Dark explains that Io appears as a globe of frosty lime green from the surface of Callisto, hence the name, which translates as "Green Moon."

PALUNGORDRA: a peculiar form of communications device known only to Thanator, and the lone example of a higher technology than that usually found in the Thanatorian cities. Captain Dark describes it as a "television crystal," and explains that the name means "the far-seeing eyes." For an account of one of the *palungordra* (the name seems to be plural) in action, see *Jandar of Callisto*, Chapter 11.

QUARRA: in *Jandar of Callisto*, this is described as a potent liquor, perhaps something like brandy.

RAMA: a color Captain Dark describes as "silver," but whether the same name is used to refer to the metal I cannot say with any surety.

RAMAVAD: Europa, the third moon of Jupiter. Captain Dark has described its appearance from the surface of Callisto as "a luminous globe of frosted azure" or "silvery blue;" but I assume that the name translates as "Silver Moon."

SORAD: a rather rare tree with crimson wood and black foliage, the reverse of which is far more common (see JARUKA).

THAD: from its use in the name *Ku Thad*, I deduce that this word means "people" in the singular. The plural form would seem to be *thana*, but this is only my conjecture.

THANATOR: the moon Callisto, a satellite of Jupiter. Terrene astronomers record that Callisto, fifth of the Jovian moons, is about 2,770 miles in diameter, 8,702 miles in circumference, and some 4,351 miles from pole to pole. Those astronomers whom I have consulted personally, at New York's Hayden Planetarium, assure me that while Callisto is one of the very largest moons in our solar system, it is far too small and has much too weak a surface gravitation to retain anything like a breathable atmosphere. As well, being more than five times farther away from the Sun than is our world, it receives a correspondingly slight amount of sunlight and heat, and should, by all accounts, be an airless and dead world, frozen in the eternal cold of space. So much for the opinions of the scientists. Captain Dark does not, to my recollection, explain the meaning of the name, but I deduce that it may be translated as *thana tor*, "world of the peoples."

THAPTOR: a beast used by the Thanatorians much as we use the horse. Captain Dark describes it as a wingless, four-legged bird about the size of a terrene horse, with a stiff rufflike mane of feathers, clawed feet spurred like those of a terrene rooster, a sharp yellow beak resembling that of a parrot, glaring eyes with orange pupils and a black iris. He further remarks that the nations of Thanator have not succeeded in fully domesticating the *thaptor,* and they retain unruly, half-wild habits (see OLO).

TOR: the Thanatorian word for "world" or "planet," combined in such agglutinating words as *Thanator* and *Gordrimator.*

UHORZ: a term which may be rendered as "indebtedness." Among the primitive Yathoon warriors, who seem generally to be devoid of the nobler sentiments and do not have any conception of friendship or love, the word *uhorz* has a very special meaning in that it is about as close to "friendship" as their barbaric mentality has been able to come.

VAD: the Thanatorian word which may best be translated as "moon," as in *Orovad,* "Green Moon." Note that the Thanatorians have only a rudimentary knowledge of astronomy, and seem to be aware only of the four satellites between their own world and its primary. But Jupiter has, in all, twelve moons, the outermost seven of which are either too small or too distant to be clearly observed from the surface of Callisto by the unaided eye.

VA LU ROKKA: a phrase which Captain Dark renders as "it was destined," and which, among the warriors of the Yathoon, expresses a fatalistic philosophy rather similar to that of the Arabic people who use the word "Kismet" to express much the same notion.

VASTODON: the elephant-boar of the Grand Kumala jungles. Insofar as Captain Dark has yet discovered, this is the largest mammal on Thanator. He describes it as having a slate-gray leathery hide, with squat, thick, columnar legs ending in flat pads, and a head like a wild boar, with vicious piglike eyes and coarse black bristles on a long, prehensile snout. It is a dangerous beast to encounter and is armed with fierce tusks of gleaming yellow ivory. Captain Dark records a hand-to-hand battle with a vastodon in *Jandar of Callisto*, Chapter 6.

YATHRIB: the dreaded dragon-cat of the jungle country. It seems a peculiar combination of tiger and reptile, its rippling catlike body clad in tough emerald scales which pale to tawny yellow at the belly plates. Its feet are armed with terrible bird-claws and a row of jagged spines line its backbone to the tip of its lashing snaky tail. Captain Dark was rescued by the Yathoon chieftain, Koja, from a monstrous yathrib as he reports in *Jandar of Callisto*, Chapter 3.

ZELL: a winged, flying reptile inhabiting the desert countries. A similar species inhabits the beaches of the two inland seas (see LAJAZELL).

The above forty-four words or terms represent all that we know of the Thanatorian language at the present time, and probably this slender sampling of the Thanatorian vocabulary is too small to serve as the basis of a scientific study of the tongue.

Any more extensive knowledge of the language, then, depends on what further information Captain Dark may give us in the future. But as communication with Callisto is erratic at best, this tantalizingly brief glossary will probably be our only source for knowledge of this, the first language of another world ever on record.

But, then, who knows what the future may yet unveil?

LIN CARTER

KURT VONNEGUT, JR.

"One of the best living American writers."

—Graham Greene

CAT'S CRADLE
A fantasy about the end of the world—replete with atomic scientists, ugly Americans, gorgeous Sex Queens, Caribbean dictators and God.

A Dell Book: $1.25
Also available as a Delta paperback: $1.95

GOD BLESS YOU, MR. ROSEWATER
A satirical and black-humored novel about Eliot Rosewater, president of the Rosewater Foundation, dedicated to bring love into the hearts of everyone.

A Dell Book: $1.25
Also available as a Delta paperback: $1.95

THE SIRENS OF TITAN
At the same time a deep and comic reflection on the human dilemma, this novel follows the richest man in America, Malachi Constant, as he gives up a life of unequaled indulgence to pursue the irresistible Sirens of Titan.

A Dell Book: $1.25
Also available as a Delta paperback: $2.25

SLAUGHTERHOUSE-5, or The Children's Crusade
A supremely unconventional war novel based on the experiences of the author as a prisoner of war during the catastrophic fire-bombing of Dresden during World War II. The hero of his story also survives the fire-bombing and is to some extent reconciled to life as it is lived on Earth. But Vonnegut is not, and in this remarkable book he has expressed his terrible outrage.

A Dell Book: 95c
Also available as a Delta paperback: $1.95

WELCOME TO THE MONKEY HOUSE
The long-awaited volume which brings together the finest of Kurt Vonnegut, Jr.'s shorter works. It is a funny, sad, explosive, wildly gyrating gathering, a mind-boggling grab bag in which every selection is a winner.

A Dell Book: $1.25
Also available as a Delta paperback: $1.95

If you cannot obtain copies of these titles from your local bookseller, just send the price (plus 15c per copy for handling and postage) to Dell Books, Post Office Box 1000, Pinebrook, N. J. 07058.

*Biggest dictionary value
ever offered in paperback!*

The Dell paperback edition of

THE AMERICAN HERITAGE
DICTIONARY
OF THE ENGLISH LANGUAGE

- Largest number of entries—55,000
- 832 pages—nearly 300 illustrations
- The only paperback dictionary with photographs

**These special features make this new, modern dictionary
clearly superior to any comparable paperback dictionary:**

- More entries and more illustrations than any other
  paperback dictionary
- The first paperback dictionary with photographs
- Words defined in modern-day language that is clear
  and precise
- Over one hundred notes on usage with more factual
  information than any comparable paperback
  dictionary
- Unique appendix of Indo-European roots
- Authoritative definitions of new words from science
  and technology
- More than one hundred illustrative quotations from
  Shakespeare to Salinger, Spenser to Sontag
- Hundreds of geographic and biographical entries
- Pictures of all the Presidents of the United States
- Locator maps for all the countries of the world

A DELL BOOK 95c

If you cannot obtain copies of this title from your local bookseller, just
send the price (plus 15c per copy for handling and postage) to Dell Books,
Post Office Box 1000, Pinebrook, N. J. 07058.

THE SENSATIONAL
WORLDWIDE BESTSELLER!
The Naked Ape
by Desmond Morris

Famed zoologist Desmond Morris will shock you with his dazzling—and witty—revelations about the human species. For man is a creature who can write immortal poetry, raise giant cities, aim for the stars, build an atomic bomb—but he is also an animal, a relative of the apes. A naked ape, in fact.

"*Whether he is discussing our origins, sex, rearing, exploration, fighting, feeding comfort or relation to other animals, he is always specific, startling, but logical. . . . He minces no words, lets us off nothing in our basic relation to the animal kingdom to which we belong.*"
—Harper's Magazine

"*A startling, novel idea, brilliantly executed. . . . To read Desmond Morris on the sex habits of the naked ape is disconcerting, to say the least. Here the detail is specific and clinical . . . and the naked ape comes out of it looking very animal indeed . . . you read on with the mixture of discovery and embarrassment . . . an enlightening, entertaining, disturbing, discomforting, ego-shrinking experience. . . . DON'T MISS IT.*"
—Saturday Review

A DELL BOOK $1.25
ALSO IN DELTA EDITION $2.25

If you cannot obtain copies of this title from your local bookseller, just send the price (plus 15c per copy for handling and postage) to Dell Books, Post Office Box 1000, Pinebrook, N. J. 07058.

"One of the 10 most notable novels of the decade."
—*Time* magazine

CATCH-22

by JOSEPH HELLER

Catch-22 is a comic novel about World War II. Set on the tiny island of Pianosa in the Mediterranean Sea, the novel is devoted to a series of impossible, illogical adventures engaged in by members of the 256th bombing squadron, an unlikely combat group whose fanatical commander, Colonel Cathcart, keeps increasing the men's quota of missions. The book's central character is Captain Yossarian, the squadron's lead bombardier. Eventually, after Cathcart has exterminated nearly all of Yossarian's buddies through suicidal missions, Yossarian decides to desert. "The best American novel to come out of World War II . . . the best American novel that has come out of anywhere in years."
—Nelson Algren, *The Nation*

Don't miss the superb
Mike Nichols film from Paramount.

A DELL BOOK $1.50

If you cannot obtain copies of this title from your local bookseller, just send the price (plus 15c per copy for handling and postage) to Dell Books, Post Office Box 1000, Pinebrook, N. J. 07058.

HOW MANY OF THESE DELL BESTSELLERS HAVE YOU READ?

1. **THE MAN WHO LOVED CAT DANCING**
   by Marilyn Durham $1.75

2. **LAST TANGO IN PARIS** by Robert Alley $1.75

3. **THE BRAND-NAME CARBOHYDRATE GRAM
   COUNTER** by Corinne T. Netzer $1.50

4. **THE EROTIC LIFE OF THE AMERICAN WIFE**
   by Natalie Gittelson $1.75

5. **GEORGE S. KAUFMAN** by Howard Teichmann $1.95

6. **THE TRUTH ABOUT WEIGHT CONTROL**
   by Dr. Neil Solomon $1.50

7. **MEAT ON THE HOOF** by Gary Shaw $1.50

8. **MAFIA, USA** by Nicholas Gage $1.75

9. **THE HAPPY HOOKER** by Xaviera Hollander $1.50

10. **THE WATER IS WIDE** by Pat Conroy $1.50

11. **THE OSTERMAN WEEKEND** by Robert Ludlum $1.50

12. **11 HARROWHOUSE** by Gerald A. Browne $1.50

13. **DISRAELI IN LOVE** by Maurice Edelman $1.50

14. **WILL THERE REALLY BE A MORNING?**
   by Frances Farmer $1.50

15. **A PSYCHIATRIST'S HEAD**
   by Martin Shepard, M.D. $1.50

16. **DEEP THROAT** by D. M. Perkins $1.50

If you cannot obtain copies of these titles from your local bookseller, just send the price (plus 15c per copy for handling and postage) to Dell Books, Post Office Box 1000, Pinebrook, N. J. 07058.